"What's going on?" he demanded.

"I'm...I'm in trouble," she stammered, trembling now from a vast array of emotions too complicated to name. "I...I shouldn't have involved you. I just...I just didn't know where else to turn. I'm afraid, Tyler. Someone is trying to kill me and I'm...I'm scared."

His hands dropped. "Who's trying to kill you?" he said at last.

"What do you care?" she managed to say.

It took him a long minute to respond, and when he did, his voice sounded almost resigned. "I just do," he said, reaching out for her again, tugging on her sleeve, pulling her gently against his rock-solid chest.

His hands holding her head, he whispered against her hair. "Heaven help me, Julie, I just do."

ALICE
SHARPE

MONTANA REFUGE

HARLEQUIN®
entertain, enrich, inspire™

This book is dedicated to Lucy Arlene with much love.

Recycling programs
for this product may
not exist in your area.

ISBN-13: 978-0-373-69659-8

MONTANA REFUGE

ABOUT THE AUTHOR

Alice Sharpe met her husband-to-be on a cold, foggy beach in Northern California. One year later they were married. Their union has survived the rearing of two children, a handful of earthquakes registering over 6.5, numerous cats and a few special dogs, the latest of which is a yellow Lab named Annie Rose. Alice and her husband now live in a small rural town in Oregon, where she devotes the majority of her time to pursuing her second love, writing.

Alice loves to hear from readers. You can write her c/o Harlequin Books, 233 Broadway, Suite 1001, New York, NY 10279. An SASE for reply is appreciated.

Books by Alice Sharpe

CAST OF CHARACTERS

Tyler Hunt—Devastated when Julie left him, he's getting on with his life until the moment she shows up again. She arrives with a story he doesn't want to hear, asking for things he doesn't want to give. It isn't long before he finds the life he made without her is as fragile as a sandcastle at high tide.

Julie Chilton Hunt—She left Tyler to find herself and landed in a dream job. Things seemed to be going well until she agreed to help a federal agent get the dirt on her boss. Now someone is trying to kill her and she's forced to seek help from the one person she has no right to ask.

Rose Hunt—Tyler's mother and the heart of the Hunt Ranch, this widow is tough as nails—usually. So what's got her on edge now?

John Smyth—This likable, helpful guy is a guest on the Hunt Ranch. So why is he always asking questions and why, when deadly things happen, is he usually missing?

James Killigrew—Julie's boss fires her in outrage when she admits she was duped. Now he's apparently looking for her. What are his intentions?

Andy—This wrangler's idea of home is a saddle atop his favorite horse. Add a thermos of coffee and now it's heaven…which he could end up visiting soon if a gunman has anything to say about it.

Nora—Julie's friend is convinced Julie has gone off the deep end. Instead of worrying about Julie, perhaps she should watch her own back.

Roger Trill—What is this lawman's goal and how many people is he willing to sacrifice to accomplish it?

Meg Petersen—A real-estate agent tickled pink to visit a genuine ranch. She's got a pretty good opinion of her skills. Is a murderer going to push them to the limit?

Red Sanders—This Boston lawyer seems to enjoy the sauce a little too much. Or does he?

Dr. Robert Marquis—An emergency-room doctor is a handy man to have along on a cattle drive. Chances are good that before this trip is over, he'll have earned his keep.

Chapter One

Julie Chilton wiped damp palms against her skirt and took a deep breath. When she spoke, her voice wavered as her vocal cords struggled with the words. "There's something I have to tell you," she said.

Her boss, Professor James Killigrew, gestured at the chair on the far side of his glass desk. "You look upset, Julie. Please, sit down."

He was a tall man with a scholarly look enhanced by glasses and tweed jackets. His high forehead ended in a shock of wild white hair but it was his voice, above all, that commanded attention. Like a fine wine holds nuances of sun, fruit and earth, his voice held intonations of wisdom, confidence and curiosity. No wonder he was so successful at supplementing his political science professor's salary with speaking engagements or that television news shows sought his on-air commentary.

That's the part of his life Julie had been hired to manage and she loved her job. Well, she had until two weeks ago....

"I don't know where to start," she confessed.

He folded his hands together and smiled encouragement. She would have given practically anything if she could have avoided this moment, but there was no choice. *Stop stalling.*

"Two weeks ago a man sat down next to me on the bus during my commute home," she began. "He showed me some identification and then started talking, his voice so soft I had to strain to hear. It was clear he knew who I was and who I worked for."

"A bus? How prosaic. And what did he say?"

"He said he was a federal agent heading a special department devoted to investigating racketeering."

Killigrew's white eyebrows shot up his forehead. "He what?"

"He showed me identification and everything. Then he told me…well, he said you were under investigation."

Killigrew's eyes widened. "Me?"

"Yes, sir. And he said because of my part in the business side of your career, I would be vulnerable for prosecution as well. Unless—"

Killigrew flattened his hands on the desktop and leaned forward. "Unless what?"

"Unless I helped him."

"Helped him what?" he said, his voice as cold as liquid nitrogen.

Julie cringed. "With his investigation. He wanted details about your upcoming trip next month, the one to Seattle. All I was supposed to do was pass along your itinerary and report incoming calls originating from there."

"And you agreed?" he said, obviously aghast. "You did this?"

Miserable, Julie nodded. "I know everything you do is on the up-and-up, Professor Killigrew," she explained. "I felt certain the agent would find that out for himself if I cooperated." She took another deep breath and added, "Okay, honestly, I was afraid your reputation would be destroyed if even a whisper of this got out, so if it could be disproven quietly, that would be best. On the flip side, what if I was wrong, what if you'd done what he said? I'd wind up in jail. And that's the ugly, selfish truth."

The next part was the hardest to admit and it required another steadying breath. "This morning, I looked in your private notebook and found a photograph."

"You looked in my notebook," he repeated, glancing down at the slender volume sitting beside his computer. He was a little old-school that way, keeping private reminders in written form and taking them with him. But this morning he'd left the book on his desk when he went to teach a class and she'd taken the opportunity to look in it.

Lot of good it had done her. Not only was his handwriting hard to decipher, but he also seemed to use some kind of shorthand code and he doodled. How many rectangles with red and yellow chevrons did one man need to draw? She hadn't even gotten to July, the month in question, when a photograph had fallen out from between the pages. One glance at that, and she'd stopped dead in her tracks.

Now she slid it out of her pocket and across the desk toward James Killigrew.

The photo was of four men in a sea of many people. They didn't even look like they were together. One was full face on, one turned to the side, another seemed to be in motion and a fourth had his mouth open as though speaking to someone off camera. One was Killigrew, two were people Julie didn't recognize and the fourth was the man who had introduced himself to her as Special Agent Roger Trill.

As her boss stared at the photo, Julie continued on. "Trill told me he'd never met you. Obviously, that's a lie.

That photo was taken earlier this year. See, you still had a beard. You shaved it off after Washington, D.C., you know where you spoke to a bunch of people about—"

"I know what I spoke about," he said coldly.

Julie swallowed. "Yes, of course you do. I called Trill's office to ask why he'd lied to me and to tell him I wasn't cooperating anymore and in fact was going to warn you about him, and that's when I found out the department he claimed to run doesn't even exist. Sir, he used me to get to you for some unexplained reason."

"Am I supposed to be grateful for this eleventh-hour spurt of candor?" Killigrew asked as he put the photo back in the book and then folded the book into the inside pocket of his tweed jacket.

"No," she said softly. "Of course not. I betrayed your trust and for that I'm sincerely sorry. In my defense, it all seemed to make sense at the time, but now I see it doesn't. I had to tell you so you could protect yourself. I'd give anything if I'd used my head to begin with."

"Are you insinuating you believe this man's story even after you know he used you?"

"No, sir, no, but he must have had some agenda and it couldn't be a good one if he went about it…this way." She had to fight the urge to lower her gaze in shame.

"Yes, you're right," he finally said. "I did need to know, mostly about the kind of woman I employ. At the very least, you are incredibly naive. The words used to describe you after that are considerably less flattering." He stood and stared down at her, his dark eyes burning. "I expect you to be out of this office within the hour."

She took a steadying breath, a protest dying on her lips. "I'll do whatever you ask. Can you just tell me who that man really is?"

"I don't have the slightest idea," he said firmly. "Now, get out."

She didn't argue.

Within a half hour, she'd dumped the contents of her desk drawer into a cardboard box and carted it outside. Not stopping for even a backward glance, she walked down the busy sidewalk wrapped in a bubble of invisibility. She'd felt this way once before in her life, a year or so ago, when she'd come face-to-face with the fact that her marriage was over.

But she wasn't in Montana anymore, she was in Portland, Oregon. Instead of high mountains and cattle trails, she now walked the city streets of the Pacific Northwest. Different climate and situation, same desolate feelings of failure and guilt.

Why had she trusted Roger Trill?

Her bus stop was up ahead and she approached it with leaden feet, pausing at the edge of a cluster of other waiting people, standing next to a woman wearing a purple scarf.

The brisk wind that blew up the gorge and over the river tangled Julie's long hair. Almost dizzy with regret, she closed her eyes until she sensed the shift of the crowd and opened them in time to find the bus approaching.

The push came from nowhere, a shove in the middle of her back that sent her catapulting into the street. The box flew from her arms as she fell and the collective gasp of the onlookers mingled with the screech of air brakes as the noise of traffic faded away.

She hit first on her knees, then her hands, her forehead banging against the pavement, coming to rest with her right cheek smashed against the road. Huge tires filled her vision. Diesel fumes scorched her throat. It was too late.

Hands grabbed her, yanked her, pulled her. The bus doors squealed open and a driver exploded from within. "What the hell?" he shouted. "You trying to kill yourself, jumping out in front of my bus like that? You crazy, lady?"

Things were fuzzy. People were picking up her belongings and putting them back in the box and it seemed unreal. Somehow she'd ended up sitting on the curb, stomach rolling, head throbbing, knees and hands embedded with gravel while her unruly hair whipped around her head.

A policeman knelt down beside her. He was in his thirties with piercing blue eyes and a fuzz of brown hair. His smile was movie star quality as he tried to reassure her.

She wasn't even sure how he got there or when. He introduced himself as Officer Yates and talked to her about a psych evaluation which wasn't surprising considering the bus driver was still telling anyone who would listen that she'd jumped in front of him.

She shook her head which made her want to throw up. "No," she said. "I was pushed."

She said it in a whisper. The policeman looked up and around and so did she. Some of the crowd had dispersed. A few remained, including the woman in the purple scarf.

The policeman questioned each of them. What had they seen or heard? Very little, it seemed. He took names and numbers. The last person he approached was the woman in the purple scarf. "I heard what she said," the woman said, nodding at Julie. "She might be right."

Officer Yates wrote on a pad. "You saw something?"

"Yes. A man in a black hoodie thing. He was standing behind her. I saw his hand come out of the pouch on the front. Now that I think about it, he might have pushed her."

"Did you see his face?"

"No. He was wearing sunglasses, that's all I can tell you."

"Young, old? Short, tall? Thin, heavy build?"

"I couldn't say about age. I'm old enough almost everyone looks young. His sunglasses were big and had those orange lenses that you don't see much anymore. He was just a medium-size guy. Oh, and he wore a silver watch."

"Do you remember anything else about the watch?"

"No, just that it was silver."

"And what did this guy do after the accident?"

"I don't know. I wasn't watching him. We were all watching her, you see. I thought for sure she was a goner. It wasn't until she was safe that I wondered about what I'd seen, but by then the man in the hoodie was gone."

The officer told the woman he'd be in touch, then he ushered Julie into his car and drove her to the emergency room where a nurse used tweezers to pick asphalt from the abrasions on her hands and knees. Next came ointments, bandages and a tetanus shot. She was asked a few questions about how many fingers the doctor held in front of her face and who was president of the United States, then she was released.

The policeman had waited for her. "I'd like you to come look at some mug shots if you're up to it," he said.

Julie blinked in confusion. "Mug shots?"

"We have a few troublemakers working this district.

Lately they've been distracting women and stealing their pocketbooks."

"And you think that's what happened to me?"

"I think it's a possibility. Maybe someone got a little too enthusiastic and pushed too hard. Then when they saw what happened to you, they were afraid to take the handbag because everyone was watching. I'll ask the other people at the stop to come down and give it a go, too. I don't suppose you can add anything to the description the older woman gave?"

"I was preoccupied," Julie mumbled. "I wasn't really paying attention."

"Well, you can do it tomorrow if you'd rather. We might get lucky."

"Might as well get it over with," Julie said.

He drove her back downtown where she carted her pitiful box of desk contents upstairs to a desk where he produced two books of mug shots and asked if she'd like something hot to drink. Julie requested coffee and he left to get it for her as she started what she suspected would be the pointless process of looking through the books. She'd been way too focused on her own problems to notice anyone but the lady in the purple scarf.

She looked around the room, wishing that the coffee would arrive as her head had begun to pound and some of the pictures in the book even blurred. Officer Yates must have gotten sidetracked.

She rubbed her temples as two men came into view walking down the hallway that ran on the other side of the interior windows. They stopped more or less across from her. Their body language caught her attention and shading her eyes, she looked at them surreptitiously through the gaps between her fingers. Whatever they were talking about had at least one of them pretty upset. She could hear a raised voice.

The man closest to her was of dark complexion and built like a linebacker. He was the one doing most of the talking, punctuating his sentences with jabs of a finger. The other man was shorter with an average build, sharp features, colorless eyes and thin lips. He wore a badge on his belt and it showed because he'd pushed his jacket aside to bury his hands in his trouser pockets.

In a world gone topsy-turvy, she recognized Roger Trill and he carried the same badge Officer Yates had shown her.

What was he doing here?

He glanced up as though sensing someone staring at him. She'd dropped her hand in surprise and their gazes locked. He appeared as shocked to see her as she was to see him.

He instantly interrupted his fellow officer and moved quickly down the hall toward the door leading into this office. Julie looked around frantically. Part of her wanted to stand her ground and demand to know what game he was playing. Another part of her, the part that relied on instinct, said get away. *Now!*

There was a second exit at the far end of the room. She grabbed her handbag from the floor and took off toward that door, scooting past people as fast as she dared, waiting for one of them to stop her. She looked back only once to see if Trill or whoever he really was, had followed. He was behind her, all right, his face set in a grim frown. She glimpsed the glint of silver on his wrist as he pushed a chair out of the way. His face was rigid with fury....

Julie exited into the stairwell and ran up a flight of stairs, sure Trill would assume she went down. She paused midstep as the door below her opened. Trill's footsteps pounded down the well as the door closed behind him. Julie resumed climbing.

She didn't know the building. She wasn't sure how to hide or how to get away. She fled to the women's restroom, but that was hardly a long-term solution. All she carried was her handbag and her only loose clothing was her now-smudged and torn raincoat. The damn thing was as red as a cape at a bullfight. Add her waist-length black hair and the fact she was five foot seven inches to say nothing of the blinding-white bandage wrapped around her head and she knew she stood out.

Looking at herself in the mirror, she chose the most obvious solution. Off came the bandage, revealing the scrapes on her forehead. She left the one covering her cheek in place as it was tinged pink in places and a bandage had to be better than blood dripping off her jaw. Up went her hair. She turned her lightweight coat inside out to reveal the tan lining and pulled the hood up over her head.

Sunglasses from the depths of her purse came next. She still looked like Julie Chilton, but maybe not if you were expecting different attire. It would have to do. It took every ounce of courage she had left to head back to the stairs.

The trip through the station was nerve-racking even though she more or less ran the whole time. Trill had pushed her in front of a bus, she was sure of it. She couldn't prove it, though, she just knew....

Somehow she reached the sidewalk without incident and crossed the street. She hurried along with her head down and caught the first city bus that came by. She didn't care about its route as long as it took her away from this area. It actually traveled past the station again and she peeked carefully through the window. Trill stood on the sidewalk, looking north and then south. As she watched, he took from his breast pocket a pair of sunglasses and perched them on his nose.

They had orange lenses.

She couldn't go to her office because James Killigrew hated the sight of her. She couldn't go home because Trill knew where she lived. She'd resided in Oregon less than a year and the one friend she'd made was a neighbor who worked swing shift at a restaurant and then checked in on her ailing brother before finally arriving home around midnight. Even if Nora was home, though, how could Julie add to her responsibilities, and how could Nora possibly help?

Whatever was going on, Julie knew she'd landed smack-dab in the middle of it. Someone wanted her dead. Why would Trill lie to her about being a policeman? Why would he try to eliminate her when she called to challenge him? For that matter, how did he know she'd called his phony office if he didn't work there? Or did he know?

How did things get to this point? What did she do now?

Chapter Two

Tyler Hunt, whistling a tune that was stuck in his head, looked up from unloading bags of grain when he heard the approach of a vehicle. An airport shuttle van rambled down the road, carrying, no doubt, either a Boston attorney named Red Sanders or a doctor by the name of Rob Marquis. Everyone else had already arrived.

The Hunt ranch was a working operation covering thousands of acres of land. Anyone who signed up for the biyearly cattle drive had to be willing to work because what went on here was the real deal. Cows and their calves had to be herded from the winter pastures in the basin up to the high mountain pastures for summer grazing; greenhorns and pros worked together to make it happen.

The shuttle stopped in the big parking area and a middle-aged man with a handlebar mustache and brand-new buckskin chaps climbed out of the back. Hard to tell which he was, a doctor or a lawyer. As the driver retrieved his suitcase, the man looked around with a big grin on his ruddy face. Tyler smiled; enthusiasm always boded well.

A slam of the door up at the house announced Tyler's mother, Rose Hunt, had also witnessed the arrival and taken time from stocking the chuck wagon to play hostess. A tiny dynamo of a woman who Tyler knew was as tough as the earth she tended, twice as strong as she looked and four times as softhearted, she walked out to the van with a little less enthusiasm than usual, exchanged pleasantries with the driver and picked up the newcomer's suitcase as the van took off back toward town.

Tyler heard the name Sanders float across the yard—the guy in the chaps had to be the lawyer—as John Smyth, another guest who had arrived earlier in the day, came out of the house. He took the suitcase from Tyler's mother, who seemed reluctant to release it. As Smyth turned to the lawyer, Rose took off toward the house. It apparently didn't occur to Red to tote his own bag. Couldn't help but wonder how a guy like that was going to handle herding cattle without someone holding his hand, but you never knew.

Smyth was a strapping, tall man in his late thirties with dark eyes, a quick wit and helpful disposition. He'd been here only a few hours, but Tyler had spotted him everywhere, talking to everyone, listening with the kind of concentration that encouraged people to open up. He seemed particularly interested in the workings of the ranch and appeared to be a natural when it came to riding and roping.

Tyler kept at the grain, whistling as he worked. There were a good dozen sacks left to unload and tote inside the barn. Rose would make the lawyer feel at home, serve him up something cold to drink, introduce him to the others, get him started with orientation. Then later Tyler would make a grand entrance and give a little pep talk.

Another vehicle caught his attention. This one was familiar, too, as it was the farrier's big white rig. Tyler had been expecting him for hours and was relieved he'd made it. One of the horses they used to pull the chuck wagon had thrown a shoe the day before, so Lenny had had to make an unscheduled visit three weeks earlier than usual. Tyler threw a sack down on top of the others and jumped out of the truck.

At six foot two inches and muscled from thirty-four years of ranch life, Tyler was a formidable man in his own right, but the farrier always made him feel like a dwarf. What everyone who met Lenny soon recognized, however, was that he had the disposition of a sweet kid. The horses loved him.

The truck stopped close by and Lenny launched his six-foot-six-inch, 250-pound frame from the cab. "Sorry I'm late," he bellowed in a deep voice that lived up to the packaging. "Got tied up over at Hidden Hollow. So, you're having trouble with Ned?"

Tyler explained about the thrown shoe.

"I'll get started on him. The rest of your string isn't due for reshoeing for almost a month. Long as I'm here, you want me to check 'em out? I'm not due at the Blister Ranch till tomorrow morning."

"Sure," Tyler said, taking off his hat and wiping his forehead with his sleeve. "You're welcome to spend the night. We can offer you a bed and a decent dinner."

"No need. You know me, I'm like a turtle, carry my little home on my back." With this he gestured at the dusty camper on the rear of his truck. Tyler wasn't altogether sure Lenny could stand up straight in the thing. Behind the truck he pulled a big trailer that he called his office. It was filled with supplies and equipment as Lenny went from ranch to ranch on a six-week cycle keeping the horses' hooves in top condition.

"Suit yourself," Tyler said, pulling his hat back on his head. "Tell me if you need anything."

"I'll just get started and, you know, let you two talk," Lenny said, his voice lower.

Tyler's brow furrowed. "What do you mean? Let who talk?"

Lenny looked back at his truck and made a little motion with his fingers. The passenger door squeaked open. The glare on the windshield had obscured the fact that Lenny had a passenger.

"I ran across her in town," Lenny said under his breath. "Because I was coming out here anyway—well, I'll just go see about Ned." He made a point of walking toward the horse barn without looking back.

Tyler's jaw literally dropped as a woman appeared. *Julie?*

For what felt like a month, they just stared at each other, he frozen to the ground, she half in and half out of the truck. He took in her sheath of glossy black hair, her deep brown eyes, the elegant features of her face. A year had passed since he'd last seen her, but right that second, it seemed like a lifetime or maybe even someone else's lifetime.

"What do you want?" he finally managed to say in a voice he didn't even recognize. It was hard to sound normal when there was a knife twisting in his heart.

That unfroze her. "Well, hello to you, too." She slammed the truck door and leaned back against it, arms held across her chest, chin up.

She'd always been on the tall, slender side, but she was really thin now, too much so. She was also beat up on her face and what he could see of her arms, like she'd been in a fight. There was something else—a furtive look, a jumpiness he'd never witnessed in her before.

Had she left him to get tangled up with some kind of vicious jerk? That was the exciting new life she'd dreamed about? The wonderful world of domestic abuse?

"I need to talk to you," she said with a defiant tone to her voice. Or maybe it wasn't defiance. Maybe it was nerves.

"I know I haven't signed the divorce papers," he told her. "I will, though. Been busy."

"It's not about that."

He turned his back on her and returned to his truck. With one leap he was in the bed again, hefting sacks of grain, moving faster now, fired up with nerves.

She followed him and then stopped. Standing a few feet away, she murmured, "It wasn't easy coming back here, you know."

"Then why did you?"

It took her a moment to answer and when she did, her voice shook. "Tyler, I've messed everything up."

He glanced at her, hoping the look in his eyes communicated the fact that he thought she was an expert at messing things up and he wasn't interested in it anymore. When she started to continue, he cut her off.

"Don't tell me, Julie. I don't care. Just leave."

Her response came quicker this time. "How do you suggest I do that? Lenny is my ride."

"Walk. Fly. You left once, you can do it again."

"Tyler, please listen to me. I need—"

He threw the bag to the ground and cut her off with a single slice of his hand. "No, you listen to me." He stopped and shook his head but didn't add anything because he didn't know what to add.

Below him, Julie rubbed her temples. The action exaggerated the sharp angles of her shoulders. He hitched his hands on his waist and stared at his boots for a second, taking deep breaths.

He had to stop acting like a hurt kid. Fact was, she couldn't walk all the way back to town and he wasn't about to be alone in a vehicle with her. He could get one of the many ranch hands to give her a ride, but looking around, he didn't see a soul.

"You can stay until Lenny leaves," he finally said. "Try to keep out of the way. We're leaving on a cattle drive in the morning and everyone is pretty damn busy."

"What about Rose?"

"My mother? What about her?"

"Maybe she could use some help."

"I doubt she wants your help," he said. In truth, his mom liked Julie and would probably love to see her, but that would just up the pressure on him to be reasonable and accommodating, neither of which he felt inclined to be, not with Julie, not now.

"I guess not," Julie said. "That's another bridge I burned, isn't it? Rose probably hates me. I shouldn't have come."

Was he curious what had brought her back? So what if he was? He'd live with not knowing. He lifted another sack and heard himself say, "Cabin eight is empty. It's yours for the night."

The relief in her voice was genuine. "Thank you." Then she added, "But Tyler, please, can't we talk for a moment?"

Bag atop his shoulder, he paused and looked down at her. "I'm very busy…"

"It'll only take a minute."

"Just stop," he said with a sarcastic laugh and a sweeping glance. "I'm not falling for that. Look at you.

You're a mess. Something bad is going on. Man trouble? New boyfriend got a temper?"

"You're acting like a jerk," she said.

"There you go. I'm a jerk. No news flash there, right?" It went against every ingrained instinct of his to turn her away, but there came a time when a man had to look after himself.

She turned with a flourish and stomped toward Lenny's truck. Maybe she planned to sit in the front seat all night. Fine with him. As he kept at his job, he saw her retrieve a large paper bag and a purse from the front seat, then walk off toward the line of pine cabins south of the main house which doubled as a lodge. She was traveling kind of light.

He looked away from her retreating form. When he heard a door close up at the cabins, he dropped the sack he held in his arms and sank onto the side of the truck bed, winded not with effort but something else, something deep inside his chest that felt as if it was sucking the breath out of his lungs.

Julie was back. And just like that, everything felt different. He rubbed his eyes and swore under his breath.

AT FIRST JULIE LOCKED the door, sat on the edge of the double bed and tried to pull herself together. Coming face-to-face with Tyler had been a lot rougher than she'd anticipated.

For two days of an endless bus ride where every stop and every new person to board loomed as a potential threat, she'd been afraid to sleep and too frazzled to eat. Getting to the ranch had been her solitary goal.

And now she was here and sure enough, just as she'd known in her heart of hearts, Tyler hated her. Couldn't stand the sight of her. Winced when he looked at her.

Damn.

She finally got to her feet and pulled the curtain aside. The blinds were open, and through them she could see that Tyler was still in the back of the big truck, hard at work.

It had been over a year since she'd seen him and time had done nothing to lessen his physical appeal. If anything, he was more dynamic than ever, his shoulders and chest broader, body leaner, face more chiseled. The ease with which he handled those fifty-pound bags of grain was remarkable and the memory of those strong arms closing around her in the dead of the night still made her ache with loss.

How could two people who were so right together also be so wrong?

She let the curtain fall back into place. She'd screwed everything up. *Everything.* What had made her think Tyler would want anything to do with her? Now what?

She finally realized she still carried the brown paper bag and set it on top of the dresser. It held the only possessions she had with her—a second pair of jeans so new they still bore their tags, underwear and a couple of T-shirts, all purchased in town before coming out to the ranch. She was down to about twenty dollars in cash and she was afraid to use her credit cards or cell phone because Roger Trill was a cop, and didn't that mean he had access to data banks and records?

She wasn't sure. She didn't know. If he was working independently from the department, if he was a crook, then maybe he would have to be cautious about drawing attention to himself. Maybe he would just cut his losses and forget about her.

She'd never talked about this ranch to anyone, not even her friendly neighbor or the other woman in the office or the lady who did her dry cleaning who was crazy about country western music and would have loved to talk about Montana. She hadn't used the name Hunt since leaving here. She'd figured if she needed so desperately to change her life, to give up what she had in order to find herself, well, then, she shouldn't rely on the past.

Gee, hadn't that worked out well?

A fresh start, that's what she'd wanted. She'd chosen Oregon because she'd never been there. She'd found the job with Dr. Killigrew almost immediately and been thrilled to discover it included occasional travel and adventure. And it paid well. She'd rented an apartment and spent her paychecks furnishing and decorating it. There wasn't one thing there that even hinted at ranch life. She'd made a place she could call a home. A fresh start. A new life.

There was a phone sitting on the nightstand, a holdover from the pre-electronic days when every room had had a land-based line. Today was a Thursday, which meant her neighbor Nora had worked the morning shift and might be away from work by now. Julie sat down on the side of the bed and placed the call. Nora picked up almost immediately and her relief at hearing the call was from Julie brought tears to Julie's eyes. *Someone still liked her.*

"I've been worried about you," Nora cried.

"I'm so sorry," Julie said. "I had to get away and there wasn't time to let you know."

"I thought something terrible had happened to you!"

"No, I'm fine."

"The police came by and got the manager to open your door in case you were inside, you know, hurt or something."

"The police?"

"Yeah. You weren't in your apartment of course, but the cop asked me a few questions about your emotional state of mind. What's going on?"

"Just a minute, Nora. Did you get a name from the policeman?"

"Yeah, Brill. No, Trill. He was really worried about you, Julie. He said they suspected you purposely stepped in front of a bus."

"No, that's not true," Julie protested.

"Are you depressed? Why didn't you come to me? What happened?"

"Nora, please listen. It didn't happen that way."

But Nora couldn't seem to stop and listen. Instead, her voice continued to grow more shrill. "Did you really run away from the police station without telling anyone? Julie, that cop made it sound like you're crazy, like you're trying to hurt yourself."

Julie clutched her stomach. Was Trill trying to set her up for a fake suicide?

"Was he alone or with other policemen?"

"Alone."

"Did you tell him anything?"

"What could I tell him? I'd been with George that afternoon and then when I got home, that policeman showed up."

Julie knew how stressful time with Nora's brother was for Nora. George was dying, and even though they tried to pretend it wasn't happening, they all knew it was. "I'm sorry I'm adding to your stress," she said. "Tell George hello for me when you see him again."

"I'll do that. I'm going back over there tonight. What the heck is going on with you? Where are you anyway?"

"That doesn't matter. Don't tell Trill you heard from me."

"But what if he comes back?"

"Play dumb. Promise me. I'll explain it when I get home."

Nora sounded worried, but she agreed. "I have your number on my caller ID," she said. "I'll call you tomorrow morning—"

"No!" Julie said. "No. I won't even be in the same state by tomorrow. Please, Nora, just don't talk about me with anyone."

"Not even your boss?"

Julie rubbed the back of her neck. "I don't have a boss. Killigrew fired me."

"Then why did he come here looking for you, too?"

Why would Killigrew travel across town to come to her apartment? "I don't know," she said truthfully.

"Is that why you were emotionally distraught? Because you got fired?"

"I'm not distraught," she insisted. "Trill is making that up."

"You sure sound like you're distraught."

"Not the way you think."

Nora was silent for a second, then she lowered her voice. "I hear a noise coming from your apartment," she said. "Just a second, I'll see what's going on."

"No—" Julie said, but Nora didn't respond. Instead, Julie heard footsteps and then a door opening. "Oh, it's you," Nora's voice said to a third party. "I wasn't expecting—"

She was cut off by a male voice and then she spoke again. "Sure, I'll be happy to help," she said. "Just give me a second to get off the phone."

The man asked her to hurry and this time he was

closer and Julie recognized the voice. Chills raced up her spine. *Trill!* As she heard the door close, she said, "Nora? What's Trill doing there?"

"He wants me to take a look in your closet and see if anything is missing."

"Nothing is missing," Julie said, "for the simple reason I didn't go home before I left."

"Well, I can't tell him I know that, can I? Not if you insist I not mention talking to you, although, listen Julie, if I did tell him you'd called, he'd stop worrying about you, right? So—"

"No," Julie said. "This is important. Don't say a word to him."

There was another pause before Nora finally responded. "Okay, but I'm worried about you. You're not acting like yourself."

Julie reassured her again and hung up.

Trill was at her apartment for a second time. What was he looking for? And what would have happened if she'd been home?

And why had Killigrew come? Maybe he'd had a chance to think and now regretted firing her. Maybe she could get her job back, make this up to him. Or maybe he just wanted to hear more about what Roger Trill had been after.

She closed her eyes. For a few hours, since arriving in Montana, she'd felt safe, as if she'd escaped. And now it seemed the trap was closing around her again....

Chapter Three

Tyler finished hauling the last sack of grain into the barn. He was so preoccupied that the last thing in the world he felt like doing was facing a room full of strangers who expected and deserved a friendly chat. He just couldn't do it. Instead, he sent Mele, one of the wranglers, to give the orientation talk. He'd make up for his no-show at suppertime.

Why had *she* come back here?

Because she's desperate. She's in trouble.

And why was that his problem? She'd stood right over there that last day and told him she felt as if she'd been swallowed by his life, she needed one of her own, she had to leave, there was no hope for them, he should forget about her and all their plans and find someone new. There would be no babies, there would be no future.

She'd cut him open and pulled out his heart.

He cleaned out a few of the horse stalls, attacking the chore like a man possessed. He was restless inside and out and couldn't wait to hit the trail. The cattle were mostly corralled nearby waiting for the morning when they'd head up toward the mountains. All day his wranglers had been giving riding and roping instructions to the guests, showing them training films, preparing them for tomorrow. The air on the ranch seemed to crackle with energy as everyone geared up for the upcoming ride.

He had a million things to do to get ready and here he was trying to come to grips with memories he'd worked a year at forgetting.

Julie.

He'd known in his heart that marrying her was a mistake. She was a town girl, her parents owned a florist shop and she'd worked in it since she was twelve. He'd looked at her work ethic and been impressed. He'd looked at her long legs and big brown eyes and been consumed with desire. She looked good, she smelled good, she'd seemed genuinely fascinated in just about every word he uttered. They'd dated through college and she'd moved out of her folks' house and onto the ranch a week after graduation, the brand-new Mrs. Tyler Hunt, exchanging one life for another.

And it had been good for a while.

Peering out the barn door, he looked toward the cabins and thought about walking up to number eight and talking to her. Hear her out. Give her advice or money or whatever she needed. Then sign the damn divorce papers and get it over with. He should have done it months before. Inertia had kept him tied to her.

He stood straight, heaved a deep breath and actually walked a step in her direction. Then he stopped. No. He couldn't do it.

SHE LOOKED OUT the window again. Tyler was nowhere to be seen.

Should she stay tucked in this room out of sight? There was an obvious allure to that plan. The four walls felt safe. Still, staring at them wasn't going to resolve anything and if the giant raw boil festering in her gut was any indication, sitting still a moment longer was going to be her undoing.

He didn't want her here, that much was clear, but maybe she could go outside for a while and just avoid him. Was her horse still on the ranch or had Tyler sold him? If Babylon was here, would Tyler come unglued if she took him out for an hour or two? Would he even have to know?

But he would; the man knew everything that went on here. The only mystery to Tyler Hunt had been his wife.

Opening the door, Julie was surprised to find the sun had dipped lower in the sky. Sunset was at eight-thirty or so this time of year, and evenings could get chilly. She went back inside and retrieved her red rain-coat which she'd spent hours on the bus repairing with a sewing kit she bought along the way. The garment was expensive, though, or had been when she bought it in a boutique. No one would mistake it for couture any-more unless they were a big fan of the pieced-together Frankenstein look.

A glance up at the mountains revealed the snow had melted, but probably not that long before. Of course it had melted; Tyler wouldn't be moving the herd if it hadn't.

She'd helped with a few of the cattle drives when they were first married five years before. Then she hadn't been able to stand being away from Tyler for very long and those nights under the stars or cuddled in his tent still awakened twinges she doubted would ever completely go away.

Sooner or later, she'd just stopped going. He'd called her spoiled and immature for not wanting to help, and she'd wanted to snap his head off. Was it immature to like different things, to want more out of life than cows and mountains?

The only one in the horse barn was Lenny, the farrier, and he was busy clipping the hooves of a palomino Julie didn't recognize. She returned his smile of greeting and walked down to Babylon's stall. Sure enough, the big red gelding was still there, his white blaze as blinding as always, his huge brown eyes alert and soft at the same time. He whinnied when he saw her and she offered him the apple she'd taken from the barrel as she entered the barn.

"How have you been?" she said as he dispatched the apple in a couple of bites. "Are you mad at me, too?"

The horse sniffed her hands for more produce and she stroked his head. "Want to sneak away for a while?"

The horse whinnied again and Julie opened the stall door. It was while she fastened a lead to his halter that she noticed a jacket hanging from a hook on the outside of the stall and beneath it, next to a stool, a pair of boots.

Her jacket, her boots, both still sitting here after a whole year as though she'd taken them off yesterday.

She looped the lead around a post and sat down on the stool, turning each boot upside down to make sure it wasn't home to a spider or two, then exchanged her casual leather shoes for the boots. They fit as they always had, like a second skin. Babylon snuffled her hair as though in approval.

Next she shook out the denim jacket and exchanged it for the red one. "I'm back, at least for tonight," she told the horse, and led him to the area they used for saddling.

Waving off the help of a new wrangler, Julie saddled Babylon before leading him out of the barn. She rode toward the river, not as comfortable and accomplished a rider as Tyler, but Babylon was an easy horse with a smooth gait and an even temperament.

She didn't need to think twice about where to head. There was one spot that had always filled her with peace when she felt this way and she headed there now. She would go to the river even though it meant riding by the century-old ranch house she and Tyler had shared during their marriage.

The house was still there, two stories of white shingles, a broad porch, barns and pastures and corrals. Tyler's truck wasn't pulled up out front and she wondered if he'd moved back to the main house after she left. The place had a deserted appearance.

Eventually, as she got closer to the river, the land began to slope gently downward until it sported underbrush, trees and wandering animal trails. She heard the rush of water before she saw it, catching sparkling glimpses through the branches as she headed to the bend where she knew a downed tree arched over the water.

This was the place on the ranch she'd missed the most, her private spot where she'd come to think and dream and work things out in her head—the one place where she could be sure to be alone.

The breeze ruffled the boughs overhead. The smell of flowers and grass chased away some of the insecurities and fears that had driven her here and she knew the sound of moving water would calm her. She pulled the horse to a stop after a while, preparing to get off and walk him down the steeper bank to water's edge, but stopped when a glimpse of something big and brown down by the river caught her eye. Her first thought was that a bear had wandered down from the mountains.

And then she realized it was a horse. Babylon sensed this, too, and made a little sound in his throat.

Her heart made a startled leap and it was a measure of where her head was that the only thought that sprang to mind was that Roger Trill had somehow teleported himself from her apartment to the river. Babylon gave a contented whinny and the horse by the river responded by tossing his head and staring up the slope.

She finally recognized Yukon, the dark gold gelding with the almost perfect white star on his forehead. Tyler's horse. Peering more closely through the trees, she glimpsed a tall figure standing atop the log, gazing downstream, apparently unaware of her presence, probably because the noise of the rushing water under the downed trunk drowned out everything else.

The sight of him standing where she'd so often sat for hours startled her. On the other hand, now was her chance. She had him cornered—he'd have to listen to her. She started to dismount and then paused.

It felt like an ambush. She'd already pushed herself on him and he'd made his feelings about her clear. Could she really confront him while he stood literally out on a limb?

What was he doing here? With a cattle drive starting in the morning, he didn't have time for idleness. Undecided about what to do, she sat there for what seemed like hours, but when he took off his hat, sat down on his heels and stared into the water as though searching for answers, she knew she couldn't encroach on his space and insist he pay attention to her. You had to ask for help, not demand it. She didn't have the right or the nerve. Even fear hadn't pushed her that far—yet.

As she turned Babylon, she spotted another rider through the trees. A man had stopped his horse farther along and seemed to be sitting astride his mount. Distance and foliage hid his identity from her, but she was almost positive she didn't know him. Dressed as he was in a Stetson and shades of browns and turned at that angle, he looked like any other cowboy.

She was afraid to take a breath, and stilled Babylon by leaning forward and running a hand down his powerful, smooth neck. "Quiet, boy," she whispered, and waited....

The stranger's attention stayed riveted on Tyler. In fact, he seemed totally oblivious to her presence and by the way he'd positioned himself, she got the distinct feeling he was doing his best to be invisible to anyone down at the river.

Julie urged Babylon forward, turning to glance over her shoulder when they broke the trees, heart drumming against her ribs as she imagined the stranger coming after her.

But he didn't.

Which raised the question: Did Tyler know he was being watched?

TYLER ARRIVED BACK at the lodge to find the guests, a couple of the wranglers and his mother seated around three of the dining room's round oak tables.

He made a quick head count and realized there was an additional person, who must have arrived while he was blowing off steam at the river. Figuring it must be the doctor they'd been expecting, Robert Marquis, he looked for the newcomer. The only one he could see was a woman of about thirty-five with dark hair and rhinestone glasses perched on a pert nose. She wore a blue neck bandanna and a red-and-white-checked shirt and was seated at a table with Red Sanders, the Boston lawyer, and John Smyth.

Well, maybe they'd gotten the name wrong. Maybe it was Roberta Marquis.

Tyler steered himself their direction and sat down at an empty place next to the woman. Across the room he saw his mother staring at him with a strained expression.

What was that about?

The easy conclusion to reach was that she'd seen Julie, although he imagined if that was true, she would have insisted she join them for dinner. Her glance seemed to stray to his left—was she staring at John Smyth?

Each table sported large platters of ham and potatoes, bowls of salads, baskets of bread, pitchers of juice and a carafe each of cabernet and chardonnay wine. Everyone helped themselves à la family-style, which they'd found over the years fostered a feeling of camaraderie that would be cemented out on the trail.

John Smyth nodded at Tyler as he scooped potatoes onto his plate.

Tyler introduced himself to the two people he'd yet to meet. The lawyer was surprisingly quiet given the flamboyance of his mustache and those buckskin chaps, but that might be explained by his frequent tips of the carafe into his wineglass. Heavy drinkers could be a problem out on the range and Tyler made a mental note to keep an eye on Red. The woman turned out to be a real estate broker from California.

"I was at a conference," the woman who introduced herself as Meg Peterson from Sherman Oaks, California, said. "You've never seen so many depressed people at one place, not ever. What with this economy…" Her voice trailed off. Tyler thought she might currently live in California, but she harbored a distinct Minnesota accent. She turned to John, her hands flying as she talked.

"I was checking out of the hotel, wishing I didn't have to go home yet," she continued, "and then the desk clerk showed me a brochure of this ranch. Why I took off right then just on the chance the ranch would have room for another guest for a few days and discovered I was in time to take part in a cattle drive!" She nodded at Tyler's mother. "That dear lady signed me right up. Rose is just a peach."

"Have you ever ridden horses or been around cattle?" Tyler asked. It was unlike Rose to agree to greenhorns with so little time to evaluate their skills and give them the basics.

"I ride all the time at home," she said. "I just couldn't be more excited if I was going to Disneyland."

"I know you'll enjoy yourself," Tyler said. He turned to Red who seemed to have fallen asleep sitting up and then to John Smyth. "You got here early this morning, Mr. Smyth. Did you find enough to do to keep you busy?"

"Call me John, please. Sure, I took a ride, saw a couple of hawks and practiced roping a sawhorse. You get the cows to stand still and I'm your man to bring them in." As Meg Peterson laughed, he smiled at his own joke, looked at Red and shrugged. Turning back to Tyler, he added, "Rose was gracious enough to let me look through some of your old picture albums when I expressed an interest in the ranch's history. It's been in your family for three generations, is that right?"

"That's right. My father's father bought it back when it was just a cattle ranch."

"I didn't see any albums of that period," Smyth said.

"There are none. A fire thirty years ago destroyed all the early records except those that we've been able to copy from county historical files."

"That's a shame."

"Yes. Well, we do have lots of photos from that point on, though."

"That you do."

John Smyth had a scar on his chin, but that kind of suited his rugged looks. In fact, up close like this, now that Tyler thought about it, Smyth looked vaguely familiar—and slightly sinister. "Have you been here before?" he asked. "Maybe on a previous vacation?"

"No, never before. I gather the decision to turn this into a guest ranch came about fifteen years ago?"

"After my father died, my mother knew she would need to switch things up if she was going to keep the ranch long enough to hand it down to me," Tyler said. "That's why you guests are so important to us. We don't make stuff up for you to do. While you're here, you're as much of a cowboy as you want to be."

Meg Peterson squealed with delight.

"Did the wranglers explain the low-stress attitude we employ to manage the livestock around here?" Tyler asked. Everyone except Red nodded. "Good. The trick is to make them want to go where we want to go. You'll get the hang of it. Be sure you get some good sleep tonight and enjoy your comfortable beds."

"Do we come back here every night?" Meg Peterson asked.

"No, ma'am, afraid not. This is a real drive. We need to get the herd up to greener pastures." The trip wouldn't really take five days if that was its only purpose and everyone knew exactly what they were doing, but you couldn't push novices too hard. Besides, it was the journey that mattered to them, not the destination.

"What about food and beds—"

"Rose takes care of the chuck wagon, right?" John Smyth said.

"Yes, Mom's handling that again this spring. Normally we leave that duty to 'Cookie' as the guys call him, though his real name is Mac, but he's off in Wyoming right now. And you'll sleep on bedrolls, but don't worry, they come with pads and a canvas flap to keep them dry. We'll hit the first camp tomorrow afternoon. There are tents available if you'd rather sleep indoors, but you might not want to miss calling it a day under more stars than you can imagine."

"I'm going to be real cowgirl by the time we get back," Meg said.

Tyler glanced at his mother's table again. She was engaged in conversation with a returning middle-aged couple named Carol and Rick Taylor who had brought along an adult son this time around, as well as with two brothers named Nigel and Vincent Creswell, both avid fishermen.

As he stared at Rose, her glance flicked his direction and then away, a frown curling the corners of her mouth.

This time he was sure of it. She'd been looking at John Smyth. Tyler served himself a slice of ham, wondering what the heck was going on.

Speaking of food, he'd have to make sure someone took something out to Julie in her cabin. No way was he going to do it. Thoughts of her killed his own appetite, but he ate anyway and did his best to keep up his end of the conversation, pleased to find the wranglers who had joined dinner service were being their usual charming selves as well, telling stories and dishing up apple pie.

His training of new cowboys and wranglers always stressed communication skills. Every moment on the ranch was a moment of someone's time and hard-earned vacation dollars. Guests were here to have fun and that meant making sure things ran smoothly. And thankfully, most of his hands were pretty good at it; they didn't last if they weren't. Truth be told, most of them got along with people better than Tyler himself did.

Dinner finally ended. One of the newest employees was a college girl studying music and she encouraged everyone to join her in the parlor for a sing-along before deep-dish apple pie and coffee were served. While the kitchen help cleared tables, Tyler took an extra plate and stacked a little of everything on it. He'd get one of the wranglers to deliver it to cabin eight.

In the kitchen he found his mother helping with the cleanup. And tucked behind the table in her old favorite spot near the fireplace sat Julie, tackling a plate of food with some of her old gusto. She flinched when she looked up and saw him.

How long had she been here? Four or five hours? But in that time, her face had acquired a little color, and the scrape on her cheek had faded. She'd found her old denim jacket, the one that hugged her breasts and nipped in the waist or had before she lost weight, and twisted what appeared to be newly showered hair into a low ponytail.

It was as if someone had turned a clock backward. She looked like his college sweetheart, like his bride, his wife. He could picture himself taking her hand, taking her back to their place, making love to her.

The knife twisted again.

"Were you trying to hide Julie away?" Rose Hunt demanded as she moved a tray of dirty dishes toward the sink. A young woman with very blond hair took it from her and as she did, a cup slid off the tray and shattered on the stone floor.

"Don't fret, Heidi, just clean it up," Rose said. "It's not like it's never happened before." Then she turned her attention back to Tyler. "Were you ever going to tell me Julie was here?"

He set the plate of food he'd assembled aside. "Probably not," he said.

"Why? You didn't sign the papers yet, did you? She's still your wife."

"Mom, this is none of your business," he said firmly. "Back to important things. Where is the doctor?"

"Dr. Marquis called to report he was having trouble getting out of Chicago," Heidi said.

"He'll arrive tomorrow morning." Rose added, "And learn as he goes. We need the business. Now, stop trying to change the subject. Everything that happens here and affects you and this ranch is my business. Imagine how I felt when I saw Julie get out of Lenny's truck but not come up to the house. I had to go get her, and then she wouldn't come into the dining room."

"I told her to leave you alone."

"Why? Do you think I can't handle reality?"

Julie cleared her throat. "Excuse me," she said, "but I'm sitting right here. Tyler didn't want to trouble you, Rose. It's as simple as that. I'll be gone tomorrow."

"So soon?"

Julie set down her fork. "Yes. I just came to talk to Tyler. I didn't know you guys were heading out with the herd. My timing sucks."

The back door opened and one of the older wranglers walked in carrying a battered-looking thermos.

"Come on in, Andy," Rose said. "You looking for some coffee?"

"You girls make the best brew on the ranch."

"And we always make extra for you," Heidi said, taking his thermos and filling it from the urn on the counter. Andy's tanned, lined face broke into a grin as he thanked them, then he turned around and saw Julie and the smile broadened.

"Well, missy," he said. "Nice to see you and that's a fact." He tipped his dusty hat and left the house. His arrival had dispelled some of the building tension—his departure brought it all back.

Rose Hunt rested her hands on her slim hips, a dishcloth dangling by her leg, her gaze directed at Tyler. "Have you two talked?"

"No."

The door behind Tyler that led to the dining room opened and John Smyth came in, holding a tray covered with dirty dishes. He paused when he saw them all standing there. Nodding at his burden, he said, "I thought I could lend a hand." He smiled at Rose, who looked away, then ambled over to the sink, set the tray down on the drain board and addressed the two women at the sink.

"Step aside, ladies. I'll wash if you two will dry."

Heidi and Melanie both laughed as Smyth plunged his hands into the dishwater.

Rose shook her head. "That isn't necessary, Mr. Smyth. You are a guest here."

"I like to pull my weight." He tossed the words over his shoulder.

Her lips thinned as she stared at his back. "I'm going to bed," she announced.

Tyler tried not to gape, but since when did Rose Hunt retire right after dinner when there were guests to be entertained and attended to? "What's wrong?" he asked. "Are you ill?"

"I may be coming down with a bug. My head hurts. And my back. I shouldn't have lifted that tray after a day spent stocking the chuck wagon. I'm not as young as I used to be. Let the kids finish the dinner chores—you two talk for God's sake. Honestly, acting like children." She slapped the cloth on the drain board for punctuation.

"I don't have time for talking," Tyler protested. "There are a million things to do before morning—"

Rose cut him off with a steely stare she'd been trotting out for years every time he did or said something she found stupid. She slid a glance at John Smyth's back, then glared at Tyler. It was clear she wanted to say something else but wouldn't in front of a guest.

Tyler glanced at Julie as Rose left the room. Julie pushed her plate away as though waiting for him to say something.

Not in that kitchen. Not with three other people washing dishes without making a sound so they could eavesdrop. No way.

"Come on," he told Julie, crossing to the door and holding it open. "Let's take a walk."

Chapter Four

The evening was chilly with a sharp bite to the wind. Julie pulled her jacket closer around herself. From a distance, she could hear cattle lowing and wondered if they sensed they'd be off on an adventure with the morning light. She used to enjoy driving the herd, especially when they finally climbed to the high pastures where the grass and wildflowers made every piece of land burst with life.

She took a deep breath that smelled like a ranch in all its hundreds of ways. She'd missed these smells and sounds more than she ever allowed herself to realize.

However, now that she was here in Montana, now that she finally had Tyler's attention, she wasn't sure what to say. She really wasn't even sure exactly what she expected him to do except maybe give some advice.

Or hide her. Maybe that's the real reason she'd come—to hide. Wouldn't he love that?

A group of guests had gathered on the wide front porch and their carefree laughter and voices floated across the still night air of the yard where she and Tyler walked. He tapped her arm to guide her away from the lights and noise. She wasn't prepared for the jolt his casual touch elicited even through layers of clothing.

"One of the wranglers mentioned you took Babylon

out this afternoon," he said as they walked along the fence that corralled some of the horses. Several trotted over to investigate, snorting and whinnying deep in their throats. Julie wasn't surprised when Tyler paused to pat a few heads.

"Is that okay with you?" she asked as a soft muzzle sniffed at her cheek.

"He's your horse."

Who was he trying to kid? Nothing on this ranch was hers anymore, not the land, not the animals and certainly not the people.

It was on the tip of her tongue to tell him about the stranger she'd observed watching him, but she didn't. It sounded so intrusive to admit she'd witnessed him out on that log. He'd been deep in thought and there was little doubt in her mind that she was the cause of his angst.

He leaned against the fence, one leg bent at the knee, elbows resting behind him on the top railing. It was too dark to see his expression, especially under the deeper shadow of his hat, but she knew him well enough to venture a guess: gaze direct, mouth in a straight line, posture casual, mind-set anything but. When he spoke, his voice was soft and brought a bittersweet wave of memories with it. "Okay, Julie, out with it. Why are you here? What's so all-fired important that coming back looks better than staying away?"

She shuffled her feet a little, then glanced up at him. "I need help."

"Money?"

"No."

"Is it a man?"

"Yes." She could almost see a knot form in his jaw, so she hastened to add, "But not in the way you're thinking."

"In what way, then?"

"The man isn't a lover or anything like that. He's a policeman—"

Tyler erupted away from the fence as though it had turned electric. Startled by his abrupt movement, a half-dozen horses whinnied and dashed back into the pasture, disappearing into the dark. "A cop?" he said. "What in the world have you been up to? I swear, if you've done anything to jeopardize this ranch—"

"If you'd signed the divorce papers when I had them sent to you, you wouldn't have to worry about your ranch!" she shot back.

"Tell me what you've done."

"You know what? Never mind. It was a mistake coming here. I'll be gone in the morning."

She turned to walk away and he caught her arm, pulling her back against him. His eyes glittered as he stared down at her.

The next thing she knew, he'd bent his head and claimed her lips, the feel of his mouth on hers achingly familiar and yet foreign. Because of their years together, she'd thought she experienced every one of his kisses— the tender, the passionate, the friendly, the ones that led to a nighttime of bliss and the ones that promised more to come. The quick ones that said goodbye for now…

But this one was different. This one was fierce, almost angry, and it shocked her down to her core.

She yanked free and took off across the yard, running blind, tears stinging her eyes.

He caught up with her up by the cabins where the shadows of the trees threw wild shapes onto the ground. Grabbing her arm again, he spun her around and gripped her shoulders. "What's going on?" he demanded.

"I'm…I'm in trouble," she stammered, trembling now from a vast array of emotions too complicated to name. Her hair had come loose of the ponytail and blew around her face and she pushed it away.

"What kind of trouble?" His voice fell to a horrified whisper as he added, "You're not pregnant, are you?"

"No, no, of course not. I…I shouldn't have involved you. I just…I just didn't know where else to turn. I'm afraid, Tyler. Someone is trying to kill me and I'm… I'm scared."

His hands dropped. "Who's trying to kill you?" he said at last.

"What do you care?" she managed to say.

It took him a long minute to respond, and when he did, his voice sounded almost resigned. "I just do," he said, reaching out for her again, tugging on her sleeve, pulling her gently against his rock-solid chest. His hands holding her head, he whispered against her hair. "Heaven help me, Julie, I just do."

HE HADN'T BEEN IN CABIN number eight for years. Many of the guests preferred staying at the lodge, although judging by the lights in the windows three or four cabins were currently populated.

When he and Julie had gotten married, they'd moved into the original old ranch house which was located closer to the river than the lodge was. He still hung his hat at the century house every night, still slept in the bed they'd once shared.

During the years they'd been together, she'd left the place much as it had always been, filled with his grandparents' furniture and knickknacks which were now antiques. Given its historical designation of "century house," the exterior couldn't be changed, but after she'd left he'd wondered why Julie hadn't made more of a mark on the interior space. If she was so determined to have a life she could call her own—one which, incidentally, did not include him—why hadn't she started with her own home? The only conclusion he could reach was that it was because he lived there, too. What she'd wanted was to be free of him.

And now she was here sitting three feet away on the edge of a bed they would never share, hair everywhere, looking as young and frightened as a wild filly. He sat down on the only chair in the room, scooting it around so he faced her. He rested his forearms on his thighs and folded his hands together. "Tell me about it," he said.

She wiped tears away with shaky fingers, casting him a wary glance as if to judge if she could really trust him. He figured she must have thought about that before now, though, or why else had she come back here? He got to his feet and walked to the window, tipping the blinds to look outside. The waxing moon had climbed high overhead.

With his back to her, she apparently felt comfortable enough to tell her story and she began talking. He heard about a job she'd been doing for the better part of a year, about the man she'd worked for, a well-respected professor. And then he heard about another man named Trill who approached her on a city bus and convinced her she should spy on her boss.

He wanted to turn around and ask if she was serious. It seemed absurd to him that she'd believed the phony federal agent.

He finally chanced eye contact when she got to the part about being shoved in front of a bus. "You're sure you were pushed?"

She nodded. "And then I saw Trill at the police

station," she added. "He matched the description the woman behind me at the bus stop gave the officer who came to help."

"So, they'd caught him?"

"No! He was a policeman."

"What did he have to say when you asked why he misrepresented himself to you?"

She rubbed her eyes. "I didn't talk to him. He tried to catch me. I…I ran away."

"You didn't ask him what the hell was going on?"

"No, I couldn't. I was so startled to see him there. And he was furious. You should have seen the expression on his face when he saw me. He chased me. I barely got out of the station."

"But that's just the point. Why did you run? You were surrounded by cops. You should have talked to the guy."

"Easy for you to say. He hadn't just tried to kill you. And then I found out from my neighbor that—"

"Wait a second," he interrupted. "You don't know for sure that's what happened. Didn't you say the attending officer mentioned attempted thefts?"

She stood abruptly. "Just stop. Let me finish before you tear me apart."

"I'm not tearing you apart," he said, bracing his hands on the back of the chair.

"Yes, you are."

"I just think it's interesting that you ran away instead of facing Trill and asking him why he pretended to be someone he wasn't. How would he have even known you knew about his deception?"

"I don't know."

"He would have had to tap your phone."

"Maybe he did."

"Why? You said your boss doesn't know him. He didn't recognize his name or his face, right?"

"Yes, but it's obvious Trill is after something."

"Exactly. And what about when this whole thing started. Why didn't you go to your boss and ask if there was any truth to these accusations instead of going behind his back? Doesn't it seem a little self-serving to you? Don't you wonder if you've developed a certain, oh, I don't know, pattern when it comes to men and rough spots?"

She stared hard at him for a moment as his last words lingered between them. Then she stood and slowly walked to the door and opened it. "I would sincerely appreciate it if you would leave," she said, looking back at him. "Without an argument, without another word."

He took a deep breath, pulled his hat on his head and did as she asked, stalking across the yard with his head down. He'd obviously hit her where it hurt and she just as obviously deserved it.

So why did he feel no sense of victory?

JULIE LAY IN BED for what seemed like hours, living and reliving every moment between dinner and falling into bed, weary beyond endurance and yet unable to so much as close her eyes because every time she did she saw Tyler's face and felt his lips and heard his voice….

He'd been talking about himself, she could see that. He was talking about the way she'd betrayed her marriage vows and run off even though she'd tried to talk to him a million times. He'd just never taken her seriously until it was too late for both of them.

And then there was that kiss and all the suppressed emotion it carried. As powerful as that had been, however, it was what came later when he pulled her into his arms and whispered against her hair that caused her throat to close now. The tenderness of his voice had been unbearable and so much more than she deserved from him.

Why did life have to be so hard?

And what did she do now? The only other people in the world she could retreat to were her parents and they were both sixty-three-year-old florists. She was a late-in-life only child and she'd always been absorbed into their lives, not the other way around. Marriage had been her way of setting herself free; that it had backfired was something her father never let her forget. So how did she slink home now and admit she'd made a mess of things? And if Roger Trill somehow followed her to Billings and found her behind the counter at The White Rose, how would she fend him off? Spritz him with flower preservative? Throw petals in his face?

Again she felt the pressure of a hand in the middle of her back followed by the smell of diesel and the sound of air brakes and the grinding of her skin against pavement....

She found she was standing and walked to the door, leaning against it and listening as though she could hear through the wooden panel. The room suddenly felt claustrophobic instead of safe, like a vault instead of a haven.

Two minutes later she'd pulled on her jeans and boots and let herself out into the night.

It was late enough that the ranch was dark and it didn't seem anything was moving, not a branch, not a molecule of air, certainly no human. Living in a city for the last year, Julie had forgotten what this kind of stillness was like, this seeming suspension of activity as still as the moment between breaths.

Tomorrow the cowboys and wranglers and guests would take off to the camp by the river. The day after that, the trail would begin to get even more remote, the countryside increasingly wild. They would travel by crystal-clear rivers and skirt craggy, desertlike plains until at last reaching the high mountain pastures where the animals would spend the summer. The calves would grow like weeds until another cattle drive in the fall brought them all back to the ranch.

She suddenly wished she was going with them, but settled for heading out to the barn, where she went straight to Babylon's stall. The horse met her at his gate with a snuffling sound of welcome and she fed him the apple she'd grabbed from the barrel.

"I'm leaving tomorrow," she told him, whispering against his nose as she ran her hands along his sleek neck. "And I want you to know I wish I wasn't in so many ways and that I'm sorry I can't be here for you."

"Then don't go," a male voice said.

Heart suddenly up in her throat, Julie jumped about a foot, turning as she did so. A tall, dark shape loomed in the deep shadows a few feet away. "Tyler?" she whispered.

"Yes," he said, advancing. He stopped right in front of her, cupped her face with his warm hands and stared down. She could see no details of his face, just the glitter in his eyes as they caught what little moonlight stole through the slats of Babylon's stable door.

"What are you doing out here?" she asked.

"Just sitting in the dark. Thinking," he said.

"What were you thinking about?"

"What do you think I was thinking about?"

"Oh, Tyler."

"I was wondering how things got to be like this, you know, between us."

"You wanted to start a family," she said, knowing it wouldn't do either one of them any good to sugarcoat the facts.

"And you didn't."

"I just wasn't ready."

"I know. I would have waited a while—"

"It was more than that. Your desire for a baby was normal and wonderful, but I knew once I was a mother there would never be a chance for me to find out about myself. I knew I'd be stuck here forever. I tried to make you understand."

He leaned closer and she felt his lips touch her forehead. "You wanted another life," he said, kissing her.

"But I wanted you to be in it."

"My life is here. You know that."

"And that's why I had to leave."

"This place has been in my family for generations," he added as though explaining himself to himself. "It's in my blood, it's the legacy for my children. It would fail if I left. I can't let that happen."

"And all that's more important than I am," she said, but this time, unlike a year before, she managed to say it without bitterness. It was a fact.

"Oh, Julie, it's not that simple," he said, his lips moving against her skin as he spoke. She turned her face upward and his lips captured hers.

This kiss wasn't confrontational like the other, but it wasn't sweet either. Julie felt like a raw wound, as vulnerable as she'd been when she hit the pavement a few days before, and as his tongue invaded her mouth, her heart seemed to explode, turning her inside out.

She ran her fingers through his hair, knocking off

his hat in the process. His hands were all over her, inciting impulses that burned every pivotal place on her body from the tips of her breasts to between her legs to deep inside her groin.

He knew her. He knew how to drive her wild with his touch, just as she knew such secrets about him. He lifted her in his arms without losing contact with her mouth and carried her along in the dark, his right arm under her bent legs, his left hand wrapped around her torso, his fingers pressing into her clothes, into her skin. And still the kisses continued, stoking the fires within, making her dizzy and disorientated.

But that wasn't true. She wasn't disorientated; she knew exactly what was on Tyler's mind, what he planned to do if she didn't stop him. Trouble was, she didn't know what she wanted.

When he knelt and laid her on a bed of clean straw and peered down at her, she reached up, grabbed the two sides of his open vest and pulled him down on top of her.

The kisses grew more and more heated as his lips traveled down her throat. She was wearing a T-shirt and he raised it, groaning when he realized she wore no bra. His mouth closed over her right nipple as his hand slipped under the waistband of her jeans, his fingers landing between her legs, his touch driving her frantic with desire.

She had to stop him. This wasn't right. Going through with this would make everything harder than ever.

But oh, the sensations, the waves of pleasure and passion. She hadn't experienced this in a year and she was overwhelmed with the desire for it to continue, to run its natural course, to be so caught up in the physicality of sex that the emotional quagmire of what it all meant would just go away.

She caught his wrist, her grip tight, and he stopped everything. Silence hung between them like a lead curtain until he said in her ear, "I want you, Julie. And you want me." As he whispered these words, he sucked on her earlobe, his hand caressing her bottom.

"No," she said, her voice so soft she could barely hear herself. "No, this isn't what I want and it's not really what you want either."

He shifted his weight, the straw rustling as he collapsed beside her. She straightened her clothes and fought to reclaim her equilibrium.

"I'm sorry—" she began, but he cut her off.

"Just don't, please. I got carried away. It won't happen again. I thought you wanted—"

"I did," she said. "But I don't."

"How do we keep screwing this up?" he added.

"I'm not sure. But I'll be gone tomorrow."

"I said you didn't have to leave."

"I know, but I think it's better if I do."

"Where will you go?"

"I'm not sure. The only thing I really know is it's not your problem. I'm not your problem."

He waited a heartbeat, then got up. Without pausing, he walked out the back of the barn, the door slamming behind him.

Chapter Five

Julie paid a last visit to Babylon before starting the walk back to her cabin. The threat of Trill and the confusion over exactly what had happened in Oregon was still ever present in her mind, heightened now by the fiasco of a few minutes before when she'd been about to make love to Tyler.

Walking with her head down to watch her step, she suddenly sensed a presence and looked up. A man stood within a pool of light out in front of the cabin next to hers, leaning against one of the porch supports, almost blending into his surroundings like a chameleon. He was as tall as Tyler, a little heavier, lighter coloring. Julie didn't recognize him and stopped dead in her tracks, a scream edging its way up her throat.

"You couldn't sleep either?" he asked, straightening up but not making a move in her direction. It was obvious he'd correctly read the alarm on her face. "I'm a guest here, too," he added. "I saw you in the kitchen after dinner. My name is John Smyth, by the way."

"Julie Chilton," she said automatically, beginning to remember him now.

"Look, I can see I startled you. I'll go back inside. We can meet again later today on the cattle drive."

"I'm not going on the cattle drive," she said, her

heartbeat back to normal. The feeling of threat had passed, replaced by something else that emanated from this man. Curiosity? Recognition? She was too upset to figure what it was. "Been standing here long?" she asked, trying to remember if she and Tyler had been noisy. She didn't think so and besides, the barn was quite a distance off.

"For a while. Well, it's time to hit the hay. I'm sorry we won't be riding the trails together tomorrow, Julie. Sleep well." He turned and walked back into his cabin, firmly shutting the door. A second later, she heard the click of a lock.

And that reminded her she'd not locked her cabin when she left it an hour before. Well, it wasn't as though she had anything worth stealing. She turned the knob and flicked on the light, turning to close and lock the door before facing her room.

Somehow, things looked different.

The fear that was always there, always waiting to erupt, came crashing back as she looked at the sack of clothes and noticed the jeans on top weren't folded the way she folded them. And hadn't her purse been lying on its side instead of standing upright? She reached for her wallet—credit cards and cash were still there. In fact, she decided as she checked everything else out, nothing seemed to be missing.

What had someone been looking for? If it was information about her, they'd seen it all, or at least everything she carried in that handbag.

The closet door was open, as was the bathroom door. She armed herself with a rod iron lamp and searched anywhere someone could be hiding and found she was alone. Then she sat down in the chair where Tyler had settled himself a couple of hours before, all the lights on, still clutching the heavy lamp, heart racing and body so pumped with adrenaline she was ready to smack anyone or anything that tried to get into her room.

Her heart about burst through her chest when she heard a knock on her door. She was instantly on her feet, clutching the heavy lamp even though her brain said bad guys didn't knock on doors.

"Who is it?" she asked, standing to the side of the door, barely breathing.

"It's Heidi, ma'am, you know, Rose's help up at the house."

"What do you want?" Julie asked.

"Rose wants to know if you could come talk to her for a few minutes," Heidi said.

"Now?"

"She said to tell you she's sorry it's so late."

It had to be important or Rose wouldn't have asked. Julie set the lamp aside and grabbed the cabin key. This time she locked the door before walking back to the house with Heidi.

TYLER WAS OUT IN THE BARN early the next morning, helping the newly arrived doctor choose a suitable mount. Dr. Robert Marquis was a tall man with a gaunt face and clothes that seemed too big for his build. More importantly, he didn't seem all that comfortable with horses and mentioned his job as an emergency room doctor in Denver several times as though depending on those laurels to cover his visible awkwardness with the animals. He all but tripped over himself when his sorrel gelding gave him a friendly nudge with his soft nose.

Tyler was anxious to get the last-minute details sewed up so they could hit the trail. He wanted to put to rest the thundering hormones and unresolved emotions that blasted around inside him like steel spheres in a pinball machine and there was no better place to do that than out herding cattle. He'd have a week to forget Julie had ever been here and then he'd sign those papers and bury a marriage that was obviously already dead.

"This one is kind of big," Dr. Marquis said, looking at the horse he'd been given with a wary eye. Seeing as he was a tall guy with minimal experience, Tyler knew the doctor needed a big, gentle horse. "Tex is a sweetheart," Tyler explained, rubbing the reddish face. "Think of him as an overgrown puppy."

Heidi showed up at the barn door, all scrubbed and smiling. "Rose wants to see you," she said.

Tyler touched his chest. "Me? Where is she?"

"Up at the house."

"What's she doing up there?" It was her job to get the chuck wagon rolling way before the rest of them hit the trail.

"I didn't ask," Heidi said. "She just told me to come get you before I laid out the breakfast buffet, so I did."

Tyler turned to the doctor. "Before you go inside and tuck into pancakes and bacon, do us all a favor and ride around in the ring for a few minutes to make sure you and Tex get along okay."

"Sure," Dr. Marquis said, casting the horse a suspicious glance. "I'm not much of a heavy eater anyway."

Tyler gave additional instructions to one of his men, then left for the house, his gaze straying only once to cabin eight.

Was Julie gone yet? Lenny had driven off bright and early; presumably, she'd left with him.

Rapping on the door of his mother's ground-floor suite, he let himself in and found her seated at the small kitchen table, still dressed in her robe, nursing a cup with a tea bag on the saucer.

"What's up?" he asked, looking around for some explanation as to why she wasn't at work.

She folded and unfolded her hands. "We may have to send everyone home," she said.

"What!"

"We'll have to refund their money and pay any travel fees they acquire," she added. "And we'll have to cancel the drive."

Tyler stared at his mother as though he was looking at a stranger. "We can't afford to do that," he said. "Anyway, the cattle need the high meadows for summer feed. What are you talking about?"

"You and the boys can drive the herd to pasture by yourselves and it won't take half the time it does with guests."

He whipped off his hat. "What's going on?" He narrowed his eyes and looked closely at her, alarmed by what he saw. Not only wasn't she dressed for work, but she didn't look so good, her skin almost as pale as her ivory robe. "What's wrong?" he demanded. "Are you sick?"

She glanced into his eyes and away, then nodded.

"What is it?"

"I'm not sure."

"What are your symptoms?"

"Don't you grill me, young man. I'm not dying, I'm just a little under the weather and worn-out."

"At the beginning of the season?"

"The beginning of the tourist season, maybe, but we had a hard winter and the calving was tough this year—on me, I mean."

"If you've been feeling sickly, then why in the world did we let Mac leave when he did?"

"His daughter's baby came early and her husband is off fighting a war. What else could we do? I just thought I could handle things, but it's become clear to me that I can't. I'm sorry, I just can't."

"Since when are you getting old?"

"Since the birthdays keep piling up."

Tyler's antenna went up again. If he didn't know better, he'd say his mother was dissembling, which was so unusual it stuck out. Rose Hunt told things as she saw them. There wasn't a beat-around-the-bush bone in her body.

And yet hadn't he noticed yesterday that she was moving a little slowly and hadn't she been untypically short-tempered the night before? This was the woman who once did a drive with a broken foot, who never quit anything, ever. If she was backing out of an obligation now knowing what it would mean to the ranch—the loss of income and reputation—then she had to be suffering. Since his father's death, Rose had been like the Rock of Gibraltar, allowing Tyler to manage the ranch as she more or less took care of their guests and the necessary staff at the lodge. She'd danced at his wedding and cried when Julie left.

If she said she was tired and feeling her age, then at the very least, she was just those things. More likely she was underplaying things rather than exaggerating them. Drat.

Perhaps he'd been leaning on her too much, asking her to be too stoic. Perhaps without knowing it he'd pushed her past her limits. "I don't know how we'll manage to pay everyone back, but your welfare comes first. We'll think of something."

"There is another option," she said.

"What kind of option?"

"Get a fill-in for me."

"Who? I can't think of anyone we can get on such short notice. I mean, we'd need someone who could manage the team and wagon as well as rustle up the kind of grub you're famous for."

"Not necessarily," she said. "Andy can drive the wagon. He was going to help me at the camp anyway, so he's a logical choice."

"Andy can make a decent cup of coffee if you don't care about stomach ulcers, but he can't cook."

"So we get someone else for that job."

Tyler thought through their current roster and tried to think of anyone, man or woman, with the skills to handle the specific requirements of cooking over open fireboxes and all the rest. He'd been trying to introduce some conveniences for food prep, things like gas burners and refrigeration, but Rose had steadfastly refused to modernize all the way.

"Someone like Julie," she added.

"Julie?" He narrowed his eyes. "Wait just a minute—"

"Let me remind you that she rode out with us for several years. She knows how to cook and manage a fire. I packed all the food yesterday and the menu is in the kitchen by the phone. Everything is ready to go."

"Julie won't do it," Tyler said. "Why should she? She didn't like helping out when she had a vested interest in the place, so why would she consent to dirty her hands now? Anyway, I think she left with Lenny—"

"No, she's still here. I spoke with her already," Rose said. "She agreed to take my place as a favor to me."

He leaned against the doorjamb and stared at her.

The feeling he was with a stranger returned full force. How could he handle seeing Julie again after what had happened the night before? "Is this all a put-on?" he asked. "Are you really sick?"

"Of course it's not a put-on. I'm just reminding you that at this late date we have two options. One, we cancel and refund. Two, Julie goes and does her best."

"So, it's a done deal. I have no choice."

Rose said nothing.

He knew they couldn't afford a loss of this magnitude. He rubbed his forehead and glanced out the window where he saw John Smyth ride by. As Tyler watched, Smyth tossed a lasso and roped a post. He got off his horse and walked up to release the rope, remounted and rode off toward the barn as though he'd been doing it his whole life.

"I bet *he* could help," Tyler mused aloud, nodding at John's retreating figure. If Andy was driving the chuck wagon, they'd be a little shorthanded on horseback. "That guy seems capable of doing anything."

"No," Rose said emphatically.

He raised his eyebrows in query, surprised at her tone of voice.

"I don't like him," she added.

"I kind of got that feeling. He seems like a nice-enough guy. What's your problem?"

"There's something about him that puts me off. I think he's trouble. You shouldn't have much to do with him."

"I've never heard you talk like that before," Tyler said. His sense of unreality was growing greater by the minute. "What's going on?"

"Nothing. Can't a person just not like another person?"

"Not when one of them is a guest of the other, paying good money for a good time," he said. "I believe I've actually heard you say as much to some of the wranglers."

She shook her head. "I'm just off-kilter right now. Let me be. What happens on the trail is your concern, not mine. Go on now, get going."

He stood and for a second wondered if it was wise to leave her to deal with this alone. Really, though, what choice did he have? The cows needed the pasture, the ranch needed the income from the guests and the guests needed him to hold things together. And there were half a dozen reliable people around the place to help her if it came to that.

"We'll miss you," Tyler said, tugging on his hat.

"You'll all be fine. Have a little faith in your wife."

His wife. That was a joke.

"See you in a week," he said.

A FEW YEARS BACK, one of the wranglers had asked if he could spend the winter rebuilding the chuck wagon. As the thing was very old and had a myriad of problems, Tyler had given the man the okay. Turned out the guy was a real craftsman and had taken the job to heart, ordering replacement pieces and adding on all the bells and whistles he could think of.

The result was beautiful and never failed to seduce guests with its charm. The natural wood pieces were shiny with varnish, while the trim had been painted a weathered-looking green. Large red wheels handled the rocky terrain with ease. The built-up back housed a dozen wooden cubbyholes and cabinets intended to hold supplies, while a table that folded down from them formed a work space. A big box below called a boot was devoted to storing cooking gear. The inside bed was empty to accommodate bedrolls, personal items and emergency supplies. The canvas awning stretched atop the bows that formed the overhead superstructure were covered with linseed oil to keep the contents dry and clean. Oak barrels for water and wooden kegs for sugar and flour were strapped along the sides.

Andy was in the front of the wagon, hooking up the horses, two big Belgium palominos named Ned and Gertie who took care of all the wagon duties on the ranch. Tyler stopped to lend a hand. "I need you to drive the team," he told Andy as he fastened the harness on Gertie.

"Me? What about Rose? She can do it. I'm assigned to help three of the guests."

"We'll have to share the load. Mom is sitting this one out."

"Who's going to cook? Me?" Andy asked, his silver gaze darting around the yard as though looking for an exit.

"No, you're just the driver," Tyler assured him as he looked up to see Julie trotting across the yard toward the wagon, buttoning her jacket as she ran. Her hair flew out behind her and caught the morning light like a raven's wing. "That's the cook."

Andy glanced over his shoulder. "Julie? I wondered why she was back. Are you and her—"

"No," Tyler said. "There is no me and her."

"You sure?"

"Yeah."

Andy finished his job and looked Tyler in the eye. "I've been here a long time, boss. I remember when you brought that little gal home after you was hitched. I never saw two people so into each other. Really surprised me when she upped and left."

"Sometimes things just don't work out," Tyler said. "You know that. You were married once, right?"

"Long time ago. But me and her was never as close as you and Julie were. My Lily wanted a whole different life."

Tyler didn't respond although the truth was that was exactly what Julie wanted, too. Ten minutes of passion in the straw wasn't going to change any of that.

"Let's get this show on the road," he said instead, and patting Gertie's golden neck, walked around to the back of the wagon where he found Julie studying the contents of the cabinet while gathering her hair into a high ponytail. She looked up as he approached.

There was something about her eyes. Dark brown like the finest chocolate or the richest coffee, they were set slightly slanted in her face making her look as though she knew a secret of some kind, something juicy and sexy, something he wanted to know. She looked at him that way now and it just about split his heart in two pieces or maybe it was the fatigue he also saw on her face, the smudges under her eyes...

She'd come to him for help and what had he done? Punished her. Turned on her. Tried to make love to her.

She cleared her throat and met his gaze. "I know my still being here is awkward and that coming along on the cattle drive is the last thing you wanted—"

"Or that you wanted," he said.

"I couldn't say no to her."

"Do you think she's really sick?"

"She's sure acting out of character. I don't know what to think."

"I don't either." He looked down at the ground to get a breather from those eyes, and then back. "Tell me the truth. Did you put her up to this so you could run away from your other problems?"

"You make it sound as if my 'problems' were a matter of late rent or something, and not fighting for my life."

He dipped his head a little, a gesture it was clear she understood implied doubt, for her eyes flashed. But when she spoke, her voice sounded resigned. "I'm sorry. I swore I was going to leave you out of this. The answer to your question is no, I am not in cahoots with Rose."

"I just wanted to know. I mean two days ago she was running around here barking out orders as usual and now she's sitting in that room of hers like she's a sick animal tucked into a cave. How could it happen that fast?"

Julie touched his arm. "She's got lots of people here to help her if she needs it and besides, everyone gets sick once in a while, right?"

He looked down at her fingers on his sleeve and wished he could touch her. Oh, hell, he wished so many things when it came to her.

"Tyler, have there been any small crimes around the ranch lately?"

He felt like she'd taken a shot at him. What was going on? "What do you mean?"

"Thefts, maybe…break-ins…" she hedged.

"Did someone steal something from you?"

"No. I don't have anything to steal."

"Then what are you talking about?"

"I was just wondering. Listen, forget it. Let's just try to stay out of each other's way, and get through this trip, okay?"

He handed her the menu list he'd found by the phone. If she could be businesslike, so could he. "It's a deal," he said. "Rose got everything ready yesterday, so you're good to go. I want you and Andy to take off as soon as you can, so you can make the river camp and get things set up. Today will be a short ride to get everyone acclimated, so we'll join you midafternoon. We've got a couple of avid fly fishermen on the ride, so maybe there will be trout for dinner."

"Same camp as before?"

"Same camp. Andy went up with me last week to check things over—he knows the way."

He knew that she knew the way, too. He wondered if she remembered the last time they'd ridden out there together, the night they'd spent...

Probably not.

Probably better that way.

Chapter Six

They left within the hour, Julie taking the time to run back to her cabin and call Nora. She couldn't stand the thought of her friend worrying about her for several days on top of her concerns for her brother and the stress of the long hours she worked. And she wanted to hear what conclusions Trill had reached the night before.

Nora didn't answer her phone, which was highly unusual as the thing was always on her body somewhere, tucked into a pocket or a handbag, connected to a headset if she was driving. She lived in constant fear she wouldn't be there for George when she needed to be. It was the main reason Julie did her best to call when Nora wasn't working because she always took her calls.

But not this time. This time the phone just rang four or five times and switched to voice mail. Julie gave a quick hearty hello and told Nora she'd be out of touch for a week and not to worry. And then she left cabin eight and went to work.

First, she acquainted herself with the supplies and ran numerous trips between the wagon and the house to ask Rose for last-minute instructions. She found a pot of beans soaking in the wagon so they'd be ready to cook later in the day, and all the usual perishables stuffed into iceboxes. Way back when, cowboys existed on beans and corn bread and whatever they could tote in a wagon—good, substantial food to be sure, but not real fancy. This trip, however, was a vacation as well as a job, and someone spending thousands of dollars expected a delicious meal at the start and finish of every day.

Julie knew from experience that Tyler had already rounded up most of the herd, but there were always last-minute details to attend to before the two hundred or so cows and calves would start the trip up into the mountains. They would follow far behind the chuck wagon to minimize dust settling on food and stores. Wranglers would help the novices get used to their horses and the rigors of the trail, but today was a purposefully slow day so as not to overtax anyone. Frankly, the pace was always pretty slow. Calves could not move that fast and the horses needed respect as well.

Groups of guests and wranglers would trade positions as the drive continued, riding drag at the back of the herd for a while, then taking on the flanks. The cows always seemed to know exactly where they were going. Tyler stressed that herding them was really just a matter of troubleshooting problems while letting them find the easiest route with a little guidance around the edges.

She'd made a human head count before they left. The menu for the night was relatively easy, but she'd been cooking for one person—herself—for the last year and her taste ran more along the line of broiled fish and steamed vegetables. No way around it, cooking rib-sticking food for almost twenty people was going to be a stretch.

She'd met all of the guests as they delivered what personal items they wanted transported that wouldn't fit in their saddlebags including their assigned bedrolls. As the wagon rumbled along the trail to the first campsite, Julie attempted to connect the names with the faces in her mind.

There was the woman with the accent riding Snow-flake, the white mare with the gray nose—Meg, no last name, please. Then there was Dr. Rob Marquis, a late arrival who appeared unaffected by a night camped out in an airport. The lawyer from Boston was named Red Sanders. Two cherubic-looking brothers from either Iowa or Idaho—she couldn't remember which—named Nigel and Vincent Cresswell. Carol and Rick Taylor were a friendly repeating husband-wife duo Julie remembered meeting three or four years back and were traveling with their grown son, Bobby. Then there were a group of three women, all secretaries at the same brokerage firm on Wall Street—Sherry, Mary and Terry. The odds of keeping their names straight were astronomical, but as they appeared to travel in a pack, it shouldn't be a problem.

That left John Smyth whom she'd met the night before and who had apparently delivered his bedroll when she was on one of her forays up to the house. It was hard not to speculate about the man. Was it possible he had searched her cabin? And if he hadn't, had he seen anyone else hanging around the cabins? She had to find a way to get him alone and ask him without involving Tyler. He'd look apoplectic when she brought up possible crime that morning and she was determined not to involve him again.

And now, here she was, sitting beside a fifty-eight-year-old grizzled cowboy with a shotgun at his feet and a six-shooter strapped to his waist. His saddled horse was tethered with a line hooking her halter to the back of the wagon. Julie almost wished Roger Trill would show up—let's see how a city cop handled the odds out here.

Andy seemed to sense she was looking at him. He grinned at her as he grabbed his thermos out from under the seat. "Boss says you and he are done," he said as the wagon dipped in a rut.

Julie took the thermos as Andy used both hands to guide the team. She hadn't expected Tyler to talk about her with his men. "Yeah," she finally said, staring toward the horizon as they traveled the worn trail through green pastures. Tiny pink wildflowers carpeted a meadow off to the left; a hawk flew circles overhead, its high-pitched call suggesting there was a nest nearby. Julie took a deep breath and for a second, it was hard to believe she'd ever been gone.

"Do me a favor, missy. Pour me a cup of that coffee, will you?"

"You still take your own thermos on horseback?" she said, amused.

"Sure. I been riding Shasta so long she knows when I grab for the thermos, her job is to move real smooth. Easier in a wagon, ain't it, Ned?"

The bigger of two gold horses tossed his head as though he'd understood Andy's comment and was agreeing.

Julie did her best to pour the coffee without spilling it. The thermos was large and old, maybe an antique, the cylinder dented from repeated falls or kicks or whatever...but the coffee that poured forth was steaming-hot and black as tar. She handed the hot cup to Andy as he bunched the reins in one hand.

"Grab yourself a mug and join me," he said, lifting the cup.

"No, thanks," she said as she screwed the top on.

"You ask me, he still misses you," Andy said after trying a sip and sighing with pleasure.

"Who misses who?" Julie asked.

"The boss. He misses you. Have to admit when I saw you last night I thought maybe you'd come back for good. You was the best thing that happened to this ranch. It was different after you left."

She looked at him again, stunned by all these revelations.

"Sure hope you think twice 'bout leaving again," he said and then held up the cup. "Okay, I know this ain't none of my business. Get bored sitting here in a wagon."

"I thought you were slated to help Rose."

"Not with the driving. Heck, she can handle a team as good as anyone. I planned on helping her once we're at camp, that's all. Like being on a horse a whole lot better."

"Then finish your coffee and stop the wagon," she said.

He did as she asked. She screwed the empty cup back onto the thermos, handed it to Andy, then jumped out and came around to his side, pausing to greet the horses as she passed in front of them. "Move over," she said, gazing up at Andy, and he did as she asked, reaching down to lend her a hand to climb back aboard.

"Teach me how to do this and then you won't have to babysit me," she said.

He flashed her another grin. "Now, missy, that ain't a bad idea, no sirree. Just coax 'em on with a gentle word or two and flip the reins easylike and they'll get going. They know what they have to do."

Julie did as directed and the team took off again. By the time they'd traveled another two or three miles, she was getting the hang of it, and by the time they'd made ten, Andy had relocated to Shasta and was riding alongside the wagon, issuing orders as needed, the disreputable thermos tucked back into his saddlebag where just the red top showed. The only rough spot came when the trail veered at a sharp angle that tilted the wagon and Julie spent a fair amount of time hanging on for dear life, hoping the horses knew what they were doing—and discovering they did.

They made the first campsite about two in the afternoon. All the camps on this ride were on Hunt ranchland except for the one two days out that crossed another rancher's land. Pains had been taken to stock each camp with necessities for the guests when possible, things like extra fishing rods, straw bales and bow and arrows for target practice. The aim, Julie knew, was to merge the spirit of a cattle drive with the comfort of a vacation, hence Rose always insisted as much be done the old-fashioned way as possible.

Because they used this camp off and on during the summer months for various trail rides originating from the Hunt ranch, it was an especially pretty one, situated as it was on a lovely piece of the river where breezes kept insects at bay and the rustling of overhead branches provided both shade and protection. The cows and horses would have to cross the river, but they'd do it upstream a ways where there were no rapids and the water was a good deal more shallow.

"Tyler and me drug the fireboxes out a couple of weeks ago," Andy said, gesturing at a duo of four-sided steel boxes each about six-feet long. He unhooked the team of horses as he added, "We brought up a load of straw bales then, too. I'll start hauling them out of the lean-to for people to sit on as soon as I get Ned and

Gertie settled over yonder. There's firewood stacked between them two trees."

"I see it," Julie said, and set about hauling wood and placing it in the firebox Tyler had welded together a few years earlier. In days past, the cook would have dug a trench and staked spit hangers in the ground, leaning over the hole. Pots would be hung from these spit hangers. But because this camp was used often and had places to store supplies, the firebox came in real handy and took away the need to dig a trench. It contained the fire and hence the danger of spreading flames and provided lots of bars and structure on which pots could be suspended and a grill laid down for cooking meat or resting a pan.

Julie found herself humming as she worked, amused when she realized it was the tune Tyler always whistled in an absentminded way. She opened up the back of the chuck wagon and hauled the iceboxes out of the bed. Andy built a more traditional campfire a short distance away, one which people could sit around once it got dark, resting on bales of straw, eating off tin plates, listening to the occasional lone coyote howl in the mountains.

Even though she had often helped Rose with these chores, she'd never been in charge of them herself. All the work kept her mind off the mess she'd made of things in Portland and even the one she'd allowed to develop the night before when her body had reacted to Tyler's touch and kisses with a mind of its own. Maybe after a week of hard work and quiet nights, she'd see a way to survive the life she'd left behind.

As she chopped onions for the beans, she looked around at the river and trees and the budding camp and realized she felt safe out here. Tomorrow, they would cross the river and begin the slow, steady climb into the mountains and with each mile, they'd be leaving civilization further behind. In the past, the journey had made her feel small and insignificant and lost somehow, but today, it seemed to promise a rebirth of sorts. All she had to do was stay out of Tyler's way.

Ham hocks, onions and seasonings went in with the beans, then Andy helped her hang the heavy pot over the fire. Along with the beans, Rose had planned on grilled steaks and chicken, corn bread, salad and berry cobbler. A coffee grinder was attached to the side of the chuck wagon, the old-fashioned kind with a hand crank, and Julie started grinding beans. Every cattle drive was run by coffee, she knew that much, and the rule of thumb was if it didn't stand a spoon on end, it wasn't strong enough.

After that she set out tubs for collecting dirty dishes. There were berries to prep, batters to measure, steak to marinate, tons of vegetables to slice. It was more cooking than Julie had done in months, but it all came back as though she'd done it yesterday, and she was actually surprised an hour later when she heard the first sounds of the approaching herd.

The cows would be kept at some distance and downwind from the camp. The wranglers—guests, too, if they liked—would take shifts keeping an all-night vigil. Cows were skitterish animals and the threat of a stampede was always a clear and present danger, so the camp was situated to offer maximum possible protection for sleeping humans.

One by one the guests started showing up on foot, their horses left to graze with the herd. The general mood was jovial and several people greeted the coffeepot like an old friend. They'd each been given lunches to carry in their saddlebags, so no one was hungry except Bobby Taylor who walked away with a couple of granola bars and the doctor who asked if there was anything to drink besides coffee. She handed him a juice box and explained there was always a stash of munchies and fruit at everyone's disposal.

"Oh, I'm not a big eater, not anymore," he said with a smile.

She wasn't sure how to react. It seemed like prying to ask what he meant, so she said, "Well, it's nice having a doctor along."

He looked up as he inserted the straw into the box. "I work in emergency and urgent care," he said, taking a couple of sips.

"That's great! If anything happens out here, it'll be right up your alley."

"Do you expect something to happen?" he asked, his gaunt face wearing an expression of alarm. He tossed the juice box into the garbage. By the thud it made, it was clear he hadn't consumed much.

"No, of course not. But you know, we're at a high altitude and even though we caution people to use sunblock, not everyone does. Occasionally there's a cut or insect bite. The cook usually hands out medical supplies like ointments and bandages."

"I brought my bag, so if there's something a little more serious, be sure you ask for help," he said.

"I will." She opened a bag in the back of the wagon and took out an apple and tossed it to him. He grinned his thanks and walked off.

The two fly-fishing brothers were soon leading a small line of fishermen, newly equipped with poles and creels, off to the river. Some of the others gathered their personal bedrolls, marked with their names, from the stack Andy had made when he helped empty the wagon. Still another group hiked off with one of the wranglers, each clutching bows and quivers of arrows.

After Julie assembled the cobbler in a couple of Dutch ovens, she adjusted the embers, trying to use twice as much heat on the lid than on the bottom. It was a tricky proposition and would be repeated with the corn bread. She'd helped do it many times, but now she was in charge and she didn't want to screw it up.

She'd just put the corn bread into another Dutch oven when she heard movement behind her and turned to find Tyler drawing himself a cup of coffee. She'd always had a weak spot for him when he was out on a ride; hard work just flattered him. And now he stood ten feet away, a coffee mug in his hand, hat pulled low over his eyes, a little dusty, a little worn, skin bronzed from the sun, gun strapped to his waist and thigh, clothes a study of tans and browns. Her knees went weak.

"How's it going?" he asked.

She knelt down and used tongs to distribute the coals on the lid. "Fine," she said, looking at her work instead of at him.

"I've been thinking about what you said this morning," he added. "About petty crime. Every situation that mixes strangers together has the potential for problems. You know that."

She kept her face turned. "Sure."

"Damn it, Julie, look at me."

She finished her job and stood, turning to face him.

"Did you have a problem last night after…well, we parted?"

"No," she said, dropping her gaze again. "No problems."

"Then why did you ask—"

"I just overheard a couple of the wranglers," she said, making things up as she went along. She was not going to involve Tyler in her problems, not again, not after last night. "They said something about a theft—"

"Wait, do you mean that situation we had last fall?"

She took a chance and nodded.

"They were talking about a kleptomaniac guest who stole things people left laying around. Her husband agreed to search her things periodically and return what she'd taken. It was really kind of sad."

Julie nodded. She'd figured every season brought some little hint of crime, and she'd been right. "Yeah, I can see how it would be," she said.

His voice reflected the fact that he considered this worry checked off on his list. "How are things going? Do you need help?"

"No, thanks."

"I could—"

"No," she said again. "Andy unpacked the bedrolls for me. I'm just getting the baking done. The beans are cooking, the salad is ready, we'll get a couple of the guests to work on hand-cranking ice cream when they get back from archery and fishing, and I'll grill the meat last thing. If I'm leaving something out, just tell me."

"Sounds like you've thought of everything," he said. "Why won't you look at me?"

She shook her head, her gaze once again averted, and walked stiffly back to the chuck wagon, her thoughts a jumble. She knew he was right behind her and she turned suddenly to ask what he wanted.

One look up at his face, and she knew what he wanted and just like that, she wanted it, too. She wanted him, and she didn't want to stop until she'd had him and that wasn't going to happen.

All the overwhelming sensations of the night before flooded through her body again and without any possibility of acting on them, she took a step backward and stumbled over an extra Dutch oven she'd left on the ground. Down she went like a bag of rocks. Tyler reached forward and tried to catch her, but her momentum pulled him along as well, and he ended up on top of her. At the same instance, she heard a whirring sound and closed her eyes, unsure what was going on except Tyler's weight pressing her into the earth had knocked her breath away.

What would she do if he kissed her right out here in the middle of the camp in broad daylight with who knows who watching?

"Julie," he said, "are you all right?"

He was getting to his feet and she opened her eyes to find him reaching down for her with one hand. He pulled her to her feet and gripped her shoulders, his gaze drilling into hers, and then it shifted to a point behind her.

"Look," he said, turning her to face the chuck wagon.

She found an arrow stuck in the frame of the chuck wagon at precisely the level of her head. It was still quivering.

She turned around to face Tyler who reached beyond her and grabbed the arrow shaft. He pulled hard, but the arrow stuck fast.

WHILE JULIE INSISTED on going back to her chores, Tyler took off toward the archery practice area. A wrangler by the name of Mele who hailed from the Big Island of Hawaii where her father owned a huge cattle ranch, conducted the lessons.

Mele was in the process of gathering the arrows by

pulling them out of the targets. Tyler took a good look around—how an arrow from this hollow made it to the chuck wagon was a total mystery.

"Where is everyone?" Tyler called when he was still ten feet away.

Mele turned and looked at him over her shoulder. He always got a kick out of how jarring this exotic-looking mix of cultures from the islands looked decked out in chaps and denim. Her slanted dark eyes smiled as she responded. "Lesson broke up a little bit ago."

He explained what had just occurred at the chuck wagon and asked her if any of the archers had acted strangely or left early.

"They may have," she said. "As long as they stay behind the line of fire, I don't pay that much attention. And before you ask, I gave them the usual lecture on safety and all of that," she added. "Really, though, I don't think any of them except John Smyth is skilled enough to shoot an arrow that far, and how would it fly over the rise of the land unless it was shot up into the air and then fell to the ground?"

"I don't think that's the case. I think it came straight at us."

"Well, John Smyth is a good shot, but Meg Peterson and Red Sanders can barely hit the target. Dr. Marquis seemed bored with the whole thing. I don't know what to tell you, but I guess it's possible someone aimed at something they weren't supposed to and the arrow went astray. Weirder things have happened."

"That's true," Tyler admitted, but hearing Smyth's named was a little jarring. His mother's warning about the man echoed in his head.

"So Smyth is a good shot?"

She pulled an arrow out of the bull's eye and nodded at the target. "Excellent."

"Did he take his bow when he left?"

"They all did." Mele narrowed her eyes. "John doesn't strike me as a careless man," she said.

"No," Tyler said. "Me either. Well, keep your eyes peeled." Turning, he walked back to the camp, making a detour by the lean-to where they stored supplies. The archery equipment was in plain view, its cupboard unlocked, the door open which wasn't unusual seeing as Mele would need to return her share of the equipment. He had no way of knowing if anything was missing or if any had been replaced, but the thought of someone running around taking potshots at Julie was a chilling thought.

Could this have anything to do with the things she'd told him about last night? Wouldn't she know if Trill was on this trip? She'd met everyone when they delivered their bedrolls to her wagon.

By the time he'd walked back to the camp, the wranglers had set up white tents for those who wanted to use them, the fishermen had returned and Julie had affixed their catch to sticks which it appeared she'd roast over the fire Indian-style. He had no idea she knew how to do that. She also had chicken quarters on the grill and was taking orders from people about how they liked their meat cooked.

The campfire was burning and the light was fading. A few people had settled on the straw bales and held cocktails in their hands. While the ranch didn't provide liquor, people were free to bring along their own personal supply if they wished. Red was one of those holding a glass and from the color of his cheeks, it wasn't his first. John Smyth sat talking to Dr. Marquis and Bobby Taylor.

Tyler heard Andy launch into a colorful trail story as he followed Julie back to the firebox where she flipped over the chicken. The Dutch ovens were off the heat and she plopped the first steak on the grill and stirred a huge pot of beans.

She looked up at him through the smoke. The fatigue he'd recognized earlier in the day was in full evidence now and he wanted to help her.

"Did you find out who—" she began.

"No," he said. "I think someone must have taken some equipment to fool around with. If he or she saw where it went and how close it came to hurting you, it probably scared the daylights out of them and they took off."

She stared at him hard for a second and he could tell she wanted to say something, but she didn't. "I hope it doesn't happen again," she said.

"It won't." He watched as she positioned the fish over the heat. "I'll give a little talk about camp safety and ask whoever shot that arrow to step forward and take responsibility."

"You can't do that," she said.

"Julie, you're lucky you tripped when you did," he said.

"I know, but—"

"I don't think you should count on luck again. If it had hit you…" he said, but then stopped with the sentence left hanging there.

She finished it for him. "It would have killed me," she said. "I know."

Chapter Seven

Julie took a steadying breath. There it was, out in the open, the thought that had been running through her mind from the first moment she saw that arrow and pictured it dripping with her blood.

Trill had found her.

But there wasn't a single person on this cattle drive who resembled Trill in any way. He simply wasn't here.

"We don't know someone in this camp even fired that arrow," she said, hating the tension she could hear in her voice. She made herself take a deep breath, and then coughed as smoke filled her lungs.

"Who else?" he insisted.

"Someone could have followed us. Anyway, look at the camp."

"What about it?"

"No, Tyler, really look. Look at your guests."

He turned as she asked and she peered through the haze between them. Almost everyone had gathered around the campfire now, sharing stories, laughing. The only ones missing were the few wranglers who were off watching the herd.

"Your guests are beginning to feel like kindred spirits," she whispered. "If you make a point of insinuating someone shot into this camp, everyone will get all awkward and look at everyone else with raised eyebrows. You'll kill their fun and on the first day of a weeklong ride, you don't want that."

"If someone tried to kill you—"

"I know, I know, I'm terrified that whatever started in Oregon has followed me out here on the trail, but we don't know for sure. It could have been a hapless mistake by an adventurous lawyer or secretary."

"But—"

"Leave the arrow where it is, right there above the coffee grinder. It won't take long before people start asking about it and I'll tell them something that makes the point about watching where you shoot without making it sound like I was a potential murder victim. Because we leave the archery equipment here when we travel on tomorrow, what difference does it make?"

"I asked Mele to try to figure out if anything is missing, but she can't," he said.

"She came by here and looked at the arrow a while back. She says it's one of ours...yours. Because the problem will go away when we head out, let's not make an issue of it."

He looked unsatisfied. There was an element of perverse pleasure in the fact that he finally believed she was in danger, but it wasn't a big one. She couldn't let him risk the whole trip because of one little thing that could have been an accident.

Or a direct attempt to kill her.

She flipped the meat and swore under her breath as she realized it was overdone. "Go away. I've got to concentrate on getting these steaks cooked. Go visit with your guests."

She saw him sit with the fishermen who were taking turns cranking the ice-cream maker. The doctor wanted to know about fording the river. There was an edge of anxiety to his voice, which was understandable given the awkward way he handled his horse.

"We'll drive the herd across about a few miles upstream," Tyler told him. It was clear the doctor wasn't the only one interested in this process as voices died down to hear better.

"What about the wagon?" Meg Peterson asked. "How is that going to get across deep water?"

"They'll cross where we cross just ahead of us. Julie is new with the team, but Andy is an old hand at this. As I'm sure most of you realize, the winter months can change things on a river, creating situations that alter from year to year. This spring I rode out and determined the best way for all of us to proceed. By the time we drive the cattle into the ravine where we'll spend the night, the cook will be there first with a pot of coffee ready and dinner under way. "Isn't that right, Julie?"

Julie waved an arm. "That's right."

"But what about lunch?" Bobby Taylor asked.

"Same as today," Julie called. "You'll carry water and food on your horse with you for lunch. But trust me, breakfast will be so filling that you won't be hungry for a while."

"I wouldn't bank on that," Bobby said, rubbing his rounded belly.

Julie rang the chow bell and all heads turned her direction. As she dished out the entrées, people helped themselves to steaming side dishes all of which were served buffet-style, right off the fire except for the salad.

Tyler came through the line and accepted the steak she served him, then ate his dinner while seated on a bale of straw talking to the woman with the thick Minnesota accent. But he excused himself as soon as dinner was over and delivered his dirty plate to the washtub where Julie had started the chore of scraping leftovers into a bin.

"You did a good job," he said. "Everything tasted great. In fact, your beans are better than my mom's, but don't tell her I said that."

"I won't. Have you heard from her?" she added, gesturing at his pocket where she knew he kept his phone.

"No reception because of the mountain," he said. "I figure if anything was too wrong, she'd send one of the wranglers after us on an ATV. To tell you the truth, I think she plain just didn't want to come."

Or she was trying to set you and me up for a little one-on-one time, Julie thought but didn't say. Instead she smiled a greeting at Andy who came up behind Tyler. He dumped his plate in the bin, then held up his thermos. "Enough for a refill?" he asked.

"Of course," she said, and took the thermos to fill it.

Tyler shifted his weight. "I have to go start my shift so someone else can get their supper. Shall I assign a couple of cowboys to help you wash—"

"No, thank you," she said, interrupting him. "Andy pumped water out of the well for me to heat for dishes. I'm all set."

"I was just trying to help," he said. "You look bushed."

"I took on this job and I'll finish it," she said, screwing the plug back into the thermos and handing it to Andy. "Your wranglers have their own chores."

Tyler held up both hands. "I wasn't implying you can't do the work—"

"Good, because I can. Go on. The sooner you get everyone back here to eat their supper, the sooner I can finish cleaning up and go to bed."

He and Andy took the hint and left together.

Julie accepted compliments on the meal from the cheerful diners as she dished out cobbler and ice cream. By now it was almost dark and the hum of the guest voices soon grew softer as though people were wearing out. Mele, the Hawaiian gal, started a song with her little ukulele for accompaniment and the juxtaposition of the stringed instrument, island melody and the Montana sky was perfect.

"Let me help," a male voice said as Julie scraped the last of the dishes. Julie recognized the tall, straight form of John Smyth as he stepped into the light cast by the lantern.

"It's okay, I'm fine," she said.

"I'll wash so you can put things away," he said, rolling up his sleeves. "I wouldn't know where things go."

Remembering she wanted to ask him about seeing anyone by her cabin the night before, she nodded. She picked up a dish towel as he handed her a cup to rinse and dry.

"Beautiful night," she said.

"Sure is." He whistled a few notes, then stopped. "I picked up that tune somewhere," he mused.

"From Tyler," she said.

"Is that where? It's catchy. Do you know what it's called?"

"I have no idea. He's whistled it as long as I can remember, though."

"Then you've known him a long time?"

"I didn't say that," she responded.

He laughed as though acknowledging they were sparring. Julie wasn't sure why, however.

"I wanted to ask you something," he added after a few moments. "I was thinking of wandering over toward the herd later and helping keep an eye on things. Do you suppose that's okay?"

"I'm sure it is," she said, emptying a kettle of hot water into the rinsing basin. The sleepless nights that had preceded this trip were beginning to catch up with her and she stifled a yawn. "Tyler usually gives people an opportunity to sign up during the afternoon. I thought he did that."

"I must have missed it," he said. "I went off on my own for a while."

She looked up quickly, her eyebrows raised. Had he been wandering around shooting arrows? "Well, just go on over," she added, pouring additional hot water into the washbasin, too. Then she filled the kettle again with well water and put it back over the flames. Five years ago, they'd used the river as a source for non-potable water, then Tyler had sunk a well making it all a lot easier.

"You do this like you were born to it," John commented.

"I've had a little experience."

"Where?" he asked.

"Here and there."

"Ever worked with Tyler before?"

She shrugged. "Some."

"How long have you know him?"

She hoped her smile was vague. "Who says I know him?"

He smiled. "There are certain…sparks…when you're together."

"Hmm," she said.

"You know, now that I think about it, I believe I heard Andy say something about your being on a cattle drive before."

She rinsed a tin plate and dried it, then set it on top of the stack of those already done. What was he fishing for? His inquiries seemed almost random, but they reminded her of Roger Trill and the way he'd wanted to know all about Professor Killigrew.

She responded to John Smyth's last question with one of her own. "I bet you were surprised to see me this morning after I told you last night I wasn't coming on the trail with you."

"No, as a matter of fact, I wasn't."

"Why not?"

"Because I got up early and ran into Rose down by the wagon. We talked for a few minutes. She said she wasn't feeling well and was going to recruit someone else to do the cooking. When I asked who, she mentioned you."

Julie looked up into his smiling eyes, not sure what to think. She accepted another plate. "Speaking of last night, did you happen to see anyone else while you were standing outside your cabin?"

"I don't think so," he said. "Why do you ask?"

"I was just wondering if there are any other restless souls I'm likely to bump into if I get up in the middle of the night to use the outhouse."

He handed her a soapy bowl and shook his head. "Not that I know of."

She couldn't come out and ask him if he'd seen anyone enter her cabin. For one thing, it would alarm him and he might talk to his fellow vacationers and the fragile sense of comradeship that was so imperative for a successful trip would blow away like a wisp of smoke. And for another, he might assume she was accusing him of tossing her room. After all, the thought had crossed her mind but she'd dismissed it. Why stand out there and announce your presence if your goal was to sneak around?

This whole thing would be different if she was a guest of the ranch and not a de facto employee…and one with an emotional connection to the boss as well. A connection this guy had picked up on, too. As it was, she had to protect Tyler if she could.

"Good to know," she said at last and was relieved when Smyth washed the last dish and left to go find Tyler.

TYLER AND ANDY KEPT the first watch, Tyler sitting atop a large flat rock, a million stars above his head. Andy was no doubt sipping a cup of joe while sitting in the saddle of his favorite horse, his favorite location in the world.

Tyler knew when his watch ended, Andy would bunk down relatively close to the herd, fearless in his way, far more comfortable with animals than humans.

An hour or two earlier, John Smyth had come to offer help and Tyler had said sure. Smyth had settled himself on the flat rock a few feet away from Tyler and talked a blue streak, but Tyler had been preoccupied with thoughts of Julie and hadn't really tracked what Smyth was saying. Smyth had apparently gotten bored because he'd left after a while, and then Tyler's horse, Yukon, showed up to pass the time before wandering off again.

Tyler looked up when he heard voices and saw a couple of his wranglers approaching. He used the light on his watch to illuminate the time. His four hours had passed amazingly fast. Usually sitting under the stars with the sounds of running water and a contented herd nearby slowed time into a peaceful, timeless tranquillity. Tonight, he'd kept seeing that arrow quivering in the post and imagining what it would have been like for it to have struck Julie instead.

He stood up and stretched out stiff muscles. One of the men took his place on the rock and Tyler started the hike back to the camp to unroll his bed and fall into a deep sleep. He was surprised to find a pool of lantern light at the chuck wagon, and veered that direction, half expecting to find Bobby Taylor helping himself to a midnight snack. But it was Julie he discovered standing at the back of the wagon.

"What are you doing?" he whispered although he could see what she was doing—chopping vegetables. It just didn't make any sense to him.

"Getting a head start on breakfast," she said softly as she sliced a red bell pepper. "Denver omelets."

"Julie, this is nuts. You need to sleep."

"No, I'm fine."

He narrowed his eyes. "Okay, what's really going on? Did something else happen?"

"Nothing. Everything is fine. I'll just finish up here and—"

"I'm not buying it," he said.

She looked around, then back at him. "Really. Go to bed. I'm okay."

"Aren't you a little nervous about spending the night alone after what happened with that arrow?" he said.

She blinked a couple of times. "No."

"Then what is it?"

She finished cutting the pepper. "I've never actually slept out on the range by myself. I don't want to bunk in the tent with the secretaries. They're guests and besides, I have to get up in four hours—"

"Julie, we both need to sleep," he interrupted, taking the knife out of her hand and setting it aside.

"Andy told me how you're learning to drive the wagon. You can't do that on a couple hours sleep and if you wanted a tent, you should have just told the guys. They would have put one up for you. You want me to treat you like my other wranglers? Then I'm ordering you to go to bed." He stared down at her and took a chance. "I'm going to bunk over there near those trees. Put the food away and come with me. It won't be the first time we spent the night under the stars together."

He shouldn't have added that last part because just like that, he could see in her eyes that she remembered the last time they'd been at this camp as well as he did. But in the next moment she yawned and he saw that fatigue coupled with fear was going to be the deciding factor.

She gathered the cut vegetables into a plastic container and deposited them in the cooler, then she grabbed her bedroll from the ground. He turned off the lantern, and using his flashlight, guided them off toward the river. He knew lying beside her was going to be exquisite torture, but he also knew he'd rather burn in hell than face rejection again. She was safe with him.

Still, he didn't want to be close to other people. He wanted her to himself, even in this limited capacity.

They both unrolled their beds on a site he'd picked out earlier, under a couple of pine trees that over the years had shed enough needles to form a springy mat on the ground. He turned off the flashlight and stripped down to his shorts, folding his jeans and shirt and placing them under his pillow.

Next to him, he could see Julie's silhouette as she

stripped down to her underwear, too, and he made himself look away.

The air was cool and it felt good to slip into the bag. Julie did the same. Her gentle sigh as she settled down floated on the still air.

If he stretched out his hand he could touch her. He wasn't going to do that, but it rattled him to realize how much he *wanted* to. Before yesterday he hadn't thought of her in weeks, he'd been fine without her, he'd consigned her to his past, and now thoughts of her and worry about her all but consumed him.

If he'd really relegated her to his past, then why hadn't he signed the divorce papers and sent them to her lawyer?

He turned his head. Her ebony hair glowed in the moonlight, so black against her pillow. He lectured himself about forbearance, trying to get comfortable while long ago images played through his mind like scenes from a movie.

Skinny-dipping in the river, making love in the water, sitting on the grassy shore and letting the summer air dry their skin, the ride back home, both of them on one horse, leading the other behind them, content just to be in each other's arms…

A breathless gasp and beating of the canvas cover next to him shattered his wandering thoughts. He sat up abruptly.

Beside him, Julie appeared to be struggling frantically to get out of her bag, slapping at the canvas cover, breathing shallow and rapid. She called his name in soft desperation. He managed to disengage himself and go to her aid, fumbling with her bag's zipper in the dark until it finally pulled down far enough for her to scramble from its confines. She tumbled over him, both of them falling to the ground in a jumble of bare legs.

"What in the hell?" he barked in a hoarse whisper, but she'd already jumped to her feet and run toward the river.

Chapter Eight

Tyler grabbed the flashlight and followed Julie as she disappeared down the sloping bank to the water. Hearing a splash, he flicked on the light and found her submerged up to her chin, brushing at herself, dipping her head beneath the surface.

The water was cold this time of year and he was startled by her behavior. What had gotten into her? He walked down to the water's edge and stood there in his bare feet, watching her.

When she started toward the shore, his heart dipped into his stomach at the sight of her emerging like a beautiful lake nymph, her face and shoulders pale next to her dark hair. She was as good as naked in this light, her breasts generous rounded globes, her hips slightly flared. His reaction to the sight of her made his voice sound cross as he said, "What in the hell are you doing?"

She came up close to him and spoke in a low voice that was hard to understand as her teeth were clattering from the cold. "Spiders, Tyler. In my bag. I was almost asleep and I felt something with my foot."

"You felt spiders?"

"Not at first. At first I felt something made of paper or cardboard. I thought maybe the cleaners had left something in the bag by mistake. It was way down at the bottom—well, you know how long these bags are so they'll work for all sizes of people. I kicked it, I guess, and then a minute later, I felt something crawl up my leg."

"Are you sure it was a spider?"

She shuddered. "I'm pretty sure."

"Come on," he said and led the way back to the bags. Tyler could see nobody else around, so apparently they hadn't made as much noise as he'd thought. "Stay back a little, I'm going to take a look," he said, taking a minute to hand her his jacket from the pile on the ground. He pulled on jeans and boots as she stood there trembling in her wet underwear and his jacket.

Using the flashlight to illuminate the bag, he pulled it open. The lining was a pale blue color, so it wasn't hard to see the small darting forms of several dark spiders scampering out of the light. Tyler managed to step on one before it got away. He took the light from Julie and sitting on his heels, bent down to look at it. Then he looked at the rest of the bag including the object Julie had hit with her foot.

When he stood up, he took a long look at her. "Come with me," he said and took off back to the river, she following behind.

"Where are we going? I'm cold," she said, her voice soft.

He addressed her from over his shoulder. "Back to the river. Remember I took that arachnology class in college?"

"Yes. Do you know what kind of spider it was that you stepped on? How did that box get in there? Don't you always launder the bags between guests?"

"Yes, we always do," he said. "Julie, take off your

clothes. I'm going to make sure you haven't been bitten."

"What?"

"That's why I brought you down here—for a little privacy. We could wake another woman to help you if you insist—"

"No, that's okay, there's no part of me you haven't seen a thousand times. But, really, I'd know if I was bitten, and so what if I was?"

"The spider I killed could have been a hobo spider. I don't think we should take a chance you would feel a bite, especially after your dip in cold water."

"You mean the kind of spider that's related to the brown recluse?"

"Yeah. I can't be certain with the naked eye, but we can't take a chance. Hand me my jacket and strip off your clothes. I'll be quick about it."

"This is not how I expected to spend my time as a camp cook," she grumbled as she took off the jacket and handed it to him. "And this is not exactly keeping you out of my problems either," she added. Facing away from him, she removed her bra and stepped out of her panties. "I'll check my front," she said, and he passed her the flashlight while he stared out at the river and tried to think of something besides the fact she was standing stark-naked eighteen inches away from him, examining her own breasts.

Finally, she handed back the light and he used it to go over her backside. He didn't touch her; it wasn't necessary, but God, he wanted to. The smooth, rounded cheeks of her butt just asked to be fondled and kissed, and as he gently lifted her hair to look at her shoulders he thought of the hundreds of times he'd done the same thing right before kissing the nape of her neck. He shone the light down her legs, wincing when he glimpsed the scabs and bruises on her knees that must be the result of hitting the pavement in front of that city bus.

The healing wounds brought home the danger she was in just like the quivering arrow had; it was all he could do not to fold her in his arms and whisk her away to safety whether she wanted it or not.

But where was safety if not out here? If he sent her away she'd be alone to face whoever was after her. If he kept her with him, she was in danger. Someone had gotten to her twice and both times, he'd been literally right by her side.

"Okay," he said at last, handing her his jacket again which she held over her chest. "I'll go get your clothes and shake them out for you."

He spent a moment checking the bag once again, fighting alarm as he noted that things had changed from just a few minutes before. He used the flashlight to scan the camp. It looked as peaceful as a camp always did this late in the night, but someone was out there, watching him. He was sure of it. He grabbed Julie's things and the rest of his stuff, shaking everything vigorously as he ran back toward the river. His breathing calmed down when he detected her willowy silhouette among the shadows.

"Here you go, guaranteed spider-free," he said, but she insisted on using the flashlight to check every inch of fabric before she dressed. He shrugged on his shirt and started buttoning it.

"I just thought of something," she said as she pulled her jeans up over her hips. "If my bag was infested, maybe the others are, too. We have to wake people—"

"No, don't worry about it," he interrupted. "That box you felt was an egg carton."

She pulled the sweater over her head and stared at him. "An egg carton?"

"And it wasn't a brand we have on the ranch, so someone had to bring it with them. But there's more. Someone cut a little vee shape on the lid over about half the cups."

"Tyler, it's like you're speaking Greek. Why was there an egg carton—"

"I think someone used it to transport the spiders to the bag."

"But the cuts—"

"Were probably how they managed to fill the cups without the spiders skittering away. Think about it, you'd have to carefully insert each spider with tweezers or something, one at a time. It's not like the others would just sit there and wait for you to close the lid.

She stared at him as though he was crazy. "Then you think someone put that egg carton half full of spiders specifically in that bag?"

"Yes. And I don't have to tell you that the bedrolls are all clearly labeled."

"But my label says Rose Hunt."

"And everyone knew Mom had convinced you to take her place."

"But even if I'd been bitten, it wouldn't have killed me straight away unless I'm allergic. I would have had time to return to the ranch—"

"Maybe. If you'd been asleep and suffered multiple bites, who knows?"

"I don't understand, Tyler," she said. "Show me—"

"I can't. The carton is gone now. So is the dead spider I stepped on."

"Gone!" she said in a whisper, turning to peer into

the dark. Her eyes were huge as she looked back at him and then toward the camp.

He put an arm around her quivering shoulder. "I'm sorry I ever doubted you," he said. "I'm sorry I didn't take you more seriously right from the beginning. You're right, someone is trying to kill you."

"And sooner or later, they'll succeed," she said.

"Not if I have anything to say about it."

THE CAMP WOULD BE USED later that week by a new group of guests that wouldn't partake in a cattle drive but would come out here for picnics and target shooting with pistols. For that reason, Tyler insisted they shake out Julie's bag, doing everything in the semidark while Julie held a flashlight.

"We can't risk anyone using it until it's examined in the light of day and cleaned," he said. Then he zeroed in on Julie and added, "Who knows you're out here? I mean besides the people at the ranch."

"No one," she said.

"Didn't you tell anyone you came from here or—"

"No, Tyler, I didn't. I used my maiden name in Oregon."

"That's fine when it comes to your friends, but when it comes to credit checks, and that includes getting a job, opening an account, renting an apartment, you had to use your legal name."

"True," she said, realizing at once that she hadn't thought of that.

"And that policeman, Roger Trill, he'd no doubt have access to your identity."

She rubbed her eyes which had gone past tired into exhaustion. "Then the answer to your questions is, everyone knows my real last name, apparently, but I never breathed a word about Montana."

"Everyone except your friends knows your name," he said as he picked up the folded bedroll and started off toward the storage shed.

"Well, there's only one woman I ever really talked to and I was sure not to tell her my real last name, not even last night when I spoke to her," Julie said as they crossed the field.

"You spoke to her last night?"

"Yes, she's a neighbor and I knew she'd be worried. I didn't tell her where I was calling from or anything and I told her not to tell anyone I called…"

"Wait a second. Who would she tell if she was your only close friend?"

"Officer Trill. He came to my apartment and convinced the super to open it. He came back while we were still on the phone. He had her convinced I was suicidal and he wanted her to check my apartment to see if anything was missing. And Nora said Professor Killigrew came looking for me, too."

"Killigrew is your boss?"

"Was my boss."

He tucked the bedding in the back of the shed. "Why didn't you tell me this last night?"

"Are you serious?" she snapped, flicking off the flashlight. She couldn't help but feel vulnerable when it shone like a beacon, pinpointing her whereabouts like a laser. "You got all huffy and judgmental. Not exactly the atmosphere for telling all, you know."

"No, I guess not," he said.

"My room was searched, too," she added. "While you and I were out in the barn…"

"That's why you brought up petty theft. Was anything taken?"

"No. John Smyth was standing outside when I came back last night. When I asked him about seeing anyone around, he claimed he didn't."

"That guy is everywhere," Tyler said. They stood facing each other in the dark for a few moments, then he added, "We have to make a decision, Julie."

"We?"

"Yes, *we.* You came to me for help and I'm finally on board with that. Now, as I see it, our options are you stay on the drive and we keep an eye on all the guests all the time. I can get the wranglers in on that without telling them why."

"Maybe it's one of the wranglers."

"One of my people? Highly unlikely. Remember the egg carton came from off the ranch and none of these guys have been away for weeks. Okay, option two is you leave tomorrow after the rest of us are already gone. I'll make sure no one follows you. You go back to our house and get the bank book, get a ride into town and take out as much as you need and then go to your parents or the police or wherever you feel safe.

"And option three is I assign someone else to continue the drive and go with you. I guess I could cancel the whole trip—"

"No, that would mean refunds. No way."

"If it would solve the problem, of course it's worth a few dollars. But if the danger lies with someone on this trip, taking them back to the ranch with us isn't going to help a lot."

She shook her head. "If those are our options, then I vote for the first one."

"Good, that's my choice, too." He closed the shed

door and added, "There's hardly any night left. Let's bunk in the chuck wagon and try to catch a little sleep."

Julie didn't want to lie that close to him, but their choices were very limited. They'd have to share his bedroll....

She was sure she wouldn't sleep a wink, not jammed up against Tyler and not after the events of the evening, but the next thing she knew, Tyler was shaking her shoulder. It was predawn and Julie guessed they'd had less than two hours of sleep. Still, she awoke with a start, instantly conscious.

"I need to go make sure everything is good with the herd," he said against her cheek, "and there was no way to get out of this bag without waking you."

"That's okay," she said, doing her best to cope with the shiver his closeness sent racing down her spine. "It's probably time for me to start cooking anyway."

"Do I have to remind you to be careful?" he asked, and just like that, her nerves stretched tight over her bones.

"No," she said, "though I'm not sure how to guard against the kind of bizarre things that are happening."

"Just be aware of your surroundings." He finally extricated himself and leaned down to lend her a hand, but she struggled without taking it. Last night had thrown them together in a nest of false intimacy. She'd fallen back into the role of his woman way too easily. He was taking things for granted and she knew she'd encouraged it, but could anything be more unfair to him than promising something she couldn't give, namely a happy-ever-after future?

He left after pulling on his boots and she climbed out of the wagon to light the lantern and start building a fire. She piled hot coals on the lid of the Dutch oven to bake the biscuits right as the sun rose in the eastern sky, spreading pale pink shadows across the land.

An hour later, guests started showing up, some moving stiffly due to the unaccustomed hours spent in a saddle the day before. Dr. Marquis walked with a stilted gait and took very small servings of the sausage biscuits and gravy, Denver omelets and fresh fruit that Julie had prepared. While everyone ate, Julie kept her hands busy packing lunches for the trail, but what she was doing underneath her calm exterior was a totally different matter.

One of these perfectly ordinary-looking people had tried to kill her—twice. And it could be any of them because they were all strangers with the exception of the returning couple. So, it could be the mild-mannered Taylors' son or the doctor, or one of the secretaries or the quiet lawyer with the flamboyant mustache, Red Sanders. Or Meg Peterson, or Nigel and Vincent, the brothers who lived to fly-fish.

Or John Smyth. The most amazing thing about both incidents yesterday was that John hadn't been around before, during or after and he *always* seemed to be around. She looked for him now and found him seated on a bale of straw next to Mary, Sherry or Terry. Whichever secretary it was, she was talking up a storm, and while John's head was bent as if he was listening, Julie could tell he wasn't. His attention seemed to be focused elsewhere and with her own gaze, she followed his line of sight to the pine trees near the river where the incident with the spiders had taken place.

And then his gaze snapped back to her. Caught staring, she produced a smile and so did he.

People started scraping their refuse into the waste barrel and depositing their plates and silverware in the dish tubs. Julie couldn't help but notice Dr. Marquis had hardly touched his food. "Sir, is there something else I could prepare for you to eat?" she asked as he slipped his plate into the sudsy dishwater.

"No, no, your meal was delicious," he said.

"I just can't help but notice how little of it you ate. I'd be happy to fix anything you like as long as we have it."

"Please don't worry about it," he said, pausing and staring at her as though gauging whether to explain. "The truth is," he said at last with a softer voice, "I had gastric bypass surgery a while back. I just fill up really fast. It has nothing to do with your cooking."

"I'm glad to hear that," Julie said.

"I'd just as soon you not mention this to anyone else," he added.

"Of course I won't. You let me know if there's something you crave, okay?"

"I will."

Tyler and a couple of the wranglers who had missed eating with the others rode back into camp a bit later as Julie washed the dishes. They kept downwind so as not to send any dirt drifting with the gentle breeze to compromise the food. Julie's gaze fastened on Tyler as he dismounted Yukon. He looked like something off the cover of a romance novel or a book about the Old West. In fact, framed as he was by other cowboys and Mother Nature, he made a timeless image, evoking the past like a print out of an old magazine.

After delivering their bedrolls to the wagon for transport to the next camp, many of the guests had left with the first group of wranglers and were now occupied in the chore of rounding up the animals. Julie needed to be long gone to stay in front of the herd.

Tyler strode over to her, questions burning in his

eyes. "Nothing has happened, everything is as normal as can be," she said, making sure her voice was soft. "Anyway, I made sandwiches out of the biscuits and sausage and eggs so you can take them with you if need be."

"We have time to sit down for a few minutes," he said as he accepted the platter of individually wrapped warm sandwiches she'd prepared. "Have you eaten?" he added.

"I had one of those," she said gesturing at the platter. "They're pretty good if I do say so myself."

He and the others helped themselves to coffee and fruit as she kept washing dishes. Andy was the first to finish his meal and once again filled his thermos from the almost-depleted urn. Then he doused the fires. Soon the other men had finished, and remounting, rode back to the herd. Tyler stopped first to stare into Julie's eyes.

"Be careful today," he said.

"Will do."

"See you in a few hours."

She nodded, alarmed when she wanted to pull him back or go with him—anything but be alone. The illusion of safety that came with his presence was definitely something she needed to fight, so she looked away from his retreating form and put away the last of the supplies.

During this time, Andy had retrieved Ned and Gertie and put them back in their harnesses. As Julie stowed the last pot in the boot and made sure all the latches were secured, he came around the wagon. "You want to drive the team out of here or shall I?" he asked.

"I'll take us as far as the river, then she's all yours," Julie said. "Do you know where we're crossing?"

"Yeah. 'Bout five or six miles upstream."

"At the fork near the split tree?"

"That's right. Okay, missy, up you go." He gave her a hand, then lowered his voice even though there wasn't anyone else around. "Boss told me what's up," he said. "No one's going to get past me and Shasta to hurt you. You can count on that."

She flashed him a grateful smile that she hoped showed faith, but the truth was she had the feeling they were dealing with a would-be killer who was determined she wouldn't live through the day.

And she didn't know why....

Chapter Nine

The ride along the river was an easy one and Julie used it to reacquaint herself with the feel of guiding the team. Andy rode behind the wagon today as though keeping watch in case someone was following them.

Julie felt safe for the moment knowing whoever was behind all these incidents had to be riding with the herd—unless there was a wild card at work in the form of a would-be killer stalking along on their own agenda. That person could be waiting up ahead for all she knew. On the other hand, the trail was far enough away from the river to reduce vegetation and that meant her line of sight was unimpaired.

Unless this person was hiding behind a rock with a high-powered rifle with a telescopic scope... It was impossible not to feel like there was a target on her forehead.

And yet, it occurred to her that all the incidents had something in common in that they were all meant to appear like an accident. There wasn't a doubt in her mind that whoever had planted the spiders had been watching from somewhere. It was pretty suspicious the way the evidence had disappeared when she'd run to the river.

It would be a lot more efficient to just shoot her or stick a knife between her ribs, but those means would announce murder. That meant her death was meant to seem accidental, the result of a foiled purse thief at a bus stop, a stray arrow or a run-in with poisonous spiders.

The trail would soon begin the descent toward the river, so Julie pulled on the reins and stopped the wagon. Ned whinnied and tossed his big head, while Gertie sniffed at the branch of a tree.

Andy once again tethered his horse's halter to the back of the wagon. He grabbed his shotgun out of its sheath and his trusty thermos and came around to climb into the wagon, stowing the shotgun beneath the seat.

He took the time to unscrew his thermos and pour himself a cup. Julie once again declined to join him, wishing she was a bigger fan of coffee because there was a chill to the morning that made her pull her denim jacket closer around her body. A jolt of caffeine couldn't help but chase away some of the latent fatigue that made the insides of her eyelids scratchy, but one look at the black brew Andy was sipping like champagne chased the temptation away.

The river was wide at this point, fanning out and running in braided rivulets separated by islands of gravel. Julie could see some white water, but it was downstream a ways where the river must get deeper as the various channels merged once again.

"Ain't much more than two-feet deep across here, but as cold as hell is hot. Melting snow, you know."

Julie recalled the dip in the river the night before—technically, earlier that day—and shivered. He was right. It was cold.

He took another swig of coffee, draining the cup and handing it to Julie so he could use both hands to take the team down a deeply rutted slope to the river beach.

She twisted the cap on the thermos and wedged it on the seat between them.

"Had us some warm days this spring," Andy said, rubbing his eyes with one fist. "Looks like there's been…been some more melting…water looks, you know…a little rougher than it did in May. Deeper, too."

"Is it safe?" she asked as she held on to the seat.

"Might be swift is all," he said. "Might get wet…"

Julie heard the effort it took for Andy to speak. He must be concentrating like mad on communicating directions via signals with the reins exactly what he wanted the team to do. She found entering the river extremely unnerving as the wagon swayed from side to side.

"Gettin'…a…little tumbly," Andy said, and added, "…mean, rocky…might roll…some…if we mit, hit, a thing…a dent…a…you know…gutter…with the treel… or a…or a…bole."

Julie looked at him, alarmed by the sound of his voice, the way he grasped for words, words that made no sense. She found his head bent forward until his chin rested on his collarbone, his eyes half-closed. She shook his arm. "Andy! What's wrong?"

His head snapped back and he looked up at her, blinking, his gaze unfocused. "Don't feel…" he stammered, and took off his hat. It immediately blew out of his hand but he didn't seem to notice.

Julie attempted to take the reins from Andy, but he wouldn't release them even though he'd slumped against her arm. "Andy, let me have the reins," she said, prying at his fingers. She looked over the side of the wagon, at the rushing water.

The reins suddenly grew slack in Andy's hands and the horses seemed to falter with the lack of direction.

She reached out to take control. Andy stood abruptly and Julie grabbed the hem of his jacket, afraid he was going to tumble overboard. He was unsteady on his feet and stumbled back to a sitting position, hitting the seat hard, sliding forward and landing on top of the reins Julie now held. That tightened the bits in the horses' mouths. Ned and Gertie lurched forward as though confused. Julie, still fighting to get Andy's deadweight off the reins and keep him from going over the front of the wagon, fell sideways with the bumpy movement, hitting the edge of the seat. She grabbed for a handhold, but the only thing she could find was the thermos, which didn't help.

Andy groaned and apparently tried to rouse himself as the horses, apparently fed up with the mixed signals, bolted for the other shore. Andy's shifting body was the final straw for Julie's delicate balance and she tripped over his torso, falling against the seat. She heard the rip of cloth and then she was falling again until she hit the water with a splash.

The wagon and horses were suddenly gone, the world reduced to two or three feet of icy-cold water. Although the current instantly swept her away, Julie wasn't too concerned. All she needed to do was grab on to the rocks on the bottom of the river to stop her momentum and stand up....

But she couldn't get a grip on the rocks, they were too covered with moss and slime and her hands slipped from their rounded surfaces. The current pushed her downstream, the river growing deeper as it went, faster, too, as the rivulets merged. Struggling to keep her head above the surface, she fought to get her legs down under her so she could stand, but she never stayed in one spot long enough to accomplish that. She swam toward the shore, but she was going very fast now and when she reached out to grab low-lying branches, the current swept her past, ripping leaves from her cold hands before she could get a good grip.

A log arching out over the water appeared up ahead. She did her best to position herself to grab it with one arm. She didn't see the broken spur extending straight out from the log until it grazed her face, almost poking out her eye. She lost the branch and was sucked under the water again. For a second, she wasn't sure which way was up. It was like being stuck inside a giant washing machine.

When she finally reached the surface again, she gasped for air and took in a mouthful of water. The river sounded different and she realized she was approaching rapids where huge rocks formed channels of their own and the river flow funneled at ever-increasing speeds through any opening it could find.

For the first time, the thought crossed her mind that she might not live through this....

TYLER TOOK HIS HAT OFF and wiped his brow with his arm. The day had grown warm, the early summer sun a shimmering light high in the blue sky.

A mile or so behind him, the herd was moseying along, guests and wranglers alike having a pretty easy ride. That would change once they got to the river. And then on the far side, the land would grow increasingly hilly and rocky making the riding trickier.

Tyler had told each of his people to keep a close eye on the guests assigned to them. Usually, with a group this small, everyone kind of looked out for everyone else, but after the things that had happened to Julie, it was clear a better method needed to be employed.

Julie and Andy would be well across the river by now, headed for the ravine. The day after, they would all start up the mountains following a trail of switchbacks that would take them into the least hospitable country of the ride. That land belonged to another rancher who had granted them the right to cross his land twice a year. Then they'd circle back to their own property and attain the meadow where the cattle would spend the summer grazing on the high mountain grasses. After a day there, they would head back.

Usually, Tyler hated to see one of these trips end, but this one was different. He wanted to find out who was trying to hurt Julie and why. He wanted to make sure whatever can of worms she inadvertently opened in Oregon got closed and sealed and buried under a ton of rocks. He wanted to let her go before he couldn't and that time was coming way faster than he was comfortable with.

He'd figured out a long time ago that he was a one-woman kind of man and since his junior year of college, that woman had been Julie. The phrase "For better or worse" had meant something to him, the vows had mattered. That they hadn't to her had been a bitter pill to swallow and he had a horrible feeling despite his best intentions to keep his feelings in check, he'd soon be choking down that same pill once again.

The river was higher than it had been when he and Andy looked at it a few weeks before, but Yukon splashed in without hesitation, crossing water and gravel bars easily. He climbed the opposite bank, following the trail the wagon must have used two hours earlier.

Tyler's first indication that something was wrong came when he saw the chuck wagon up ahead. Why had they stopped here and in the middle of the trail instead of going on to the camp? Urging Yukon forward, he arrived a minute later. He tied the horse next to Shasta and walked around to the front of the wagon, his senses on full alert, the silence unnerving.

Andy lay half on the seat, half off it, face up, mouth open, eyes closed. Ned and Gertie whinnied greetings, then went back to nosing the grass, unconcerned about the human drama going on behind them. Tyler took a minute to scan the area, calling Julie's name, listening for a response and hearing nothing but the river.

He climbed into the wagon and put two fingers against the pulse point in the older man's throat. His pulse seemed steady, but no amount of gentle patting or calling his name roused him. Tyler finally settled on getting Andy out of the wagon and placing him on the ground in the shade of a tree.

Where was Julie? He got back in the wagon and checked under the cover, but the wagon was loaded with bedrolls and supplies and nothing more. He stood on the seat for a moment, using the higher vantage point to scout the surrounding countryside, but the fact was, Julie just wasn't anywhere around.

What was going on?

Grabbing the seat, he started to get down and that's when he found a scrap of light blue denim caught in the edge of the seat where a bit of metal had snagged it. Andy was wearing shades of brown, but Julie had been wearing faded jeans and her old washed-out denim jacket when he saw her last....

"Julie," he yelled, and then he yelled her name again, looking every which way and finding no trace of movement.

Sitting down, he took up the reins and moved the rig and horses off the trail so the cattle wouldn't run over it when they came up the bank, then he made himself take the time to get Ned and Gertie out of their harnesses. He stretched a rope between two trees and tied each horse to the rope.

He worked with his heart lodged in his throat, trying to figure out what had happened to Julie. He reached a couple of conclusions. If she'd tried to come back to the herd for help because of Andy, she wouldn't have left him in the wagon, nor would she have walked. She would have taken Shasta. If that scrap belonged to her, she'd probably lost it today, which might mean she fell. If she'd fallen along the trail, he would have found her already. But if she'd fallen into the water, she might have been pulled downstream by the current. He felt the horses' legs—they were barely damp. This had all happened a while ago....

He made one last check on Andy, made sure his handgun was loaded and jumped on Yukon. He rode back to the river in a hurry, stopping the horse on the mid sandbar, looking downstream. There was no indication that anything was wrong, but no sign of Julie either on the shore or in the water.

"Come on," he urged the horse, who began walking down the middle of the river. But it soon got pretty deep and while a horse could swim, swimming downstream didn't make a whole lot of sense. He crossed to the bank again and got off Yukon. He would walk and lead the horse when he couldn't see the bank, and when he could he would ride. If Julie was here he would find her.

But, of course, it was possible she'd been taken from the wagon by another person who had ridden off with her to parts unknown. It was possible no one on the cattle drive had anything to do with the incidents of the day before, that there was an unknown force at work.

First he'd check the river and if that didn't pan out, he'd start in at the wagon and look for tracks. For a second he was torn—if the herd arrived, any tracks would be obliterated by cattle and horses, and he slowed down, undecided.

There came a time when you had to trust your gut. Anyone who worked around thousand-pound animals knew that. And his gut said travel the river back as far as he could. If she'd been nabbed, she was probably dead by now. If she was in the river, she needed him to get her out.

He comforted himself with the fact that his decision was the logical choice given that Andy didn't look like he was a victim of an ambush. Maybe he'd had a stroke or a heart attack when Julie fell.

"Julie!" Tyler yelled. He led Yukon down toward the water, then back up the bank when the way became too densely wooded, looking for some sign of her. The water was snow runoff and cold and the real danger of hypothermia was a consideration as well.

"Julie!"

What if she'd come out of the water on the other side? Well, he'd cross that bridge when and if he came to it. He got back on Yukon who picked his way over the uneven terrain while Tyler's gaze darted back and forth across the river.

He was suddenly aware that the sound of rushing water was louder than it had been before and knew it meant the river was approaching the rapids that preceded the calmer water beyond. The land itself suddenly changed, becoming steeper and so cluttered with fallen trees and rampant undergrowth that there was no way for a horse to manage it. He got off Yukon again, left him standing in a safe spot and walked to the water's edge.

The sun was even higher in the sky, the light clear, the air cool next to the rushing river. He scrambled to the top of a large rock and shaded his eyes, looking upriver and down, scanning both shores, the rapids so nearby now that their noise filled his head.

At first he didn't see anything but big dark rocks, wet with splashed water. And then he saw what at first glance appeared to be a shadow, but upon closer scrutiny, turned into a human shape—Julie's shape.

"Julie!" he yelled, and miracle of miracles, she slowly sat up and turned to face him.

She'd ended up atop a rock in the middle of the river, surrounded by white water.

He saw her mouth move, but her voice was swallowed by the sound. "Stay where you are!" he yelled, uncertain she heard him, but really, what choice did she have? He'd bet money that that rock was as slippery as a peeled avocado. There was no way for her to jump from it to the one closer to shore, a distance of at least five feet. He ran back up the bank and grabbed his lasso from Yukon's saddle, then ran along the river until he was opposite her.

Moving quickly, he balanced himself on the rocks, the leather soles of his boots finding safe passage, until he was standing on the rock closest to her position. He held up the lasso and he saw her nod. Now that he was closer, he could see that she was afraid to stand, afraid she might fall again.

He twirled the rope and threw it and it slipped right over her shoulders as if she were a calf at branding time. With one hand, she guided it down to her waist and held on to it. Even from this distance he could see her chin quivering with cold.

Moving backward, he looped his end of the rope around a tree trunk and then gave her a thumbs-up gesture.

What courage it must have taken for her to slip into that water again. She was instantly tugged downstream, her head disappearing, but there was no way in hell he was going to lose her now, pulling harder than he ever had in his life. She finally got close enough to the shore where the water calmed down and still keeping a purchase on the rope, he reached out a hand and she grabbed it.

A moment later, he'd hauled her out of the water and she fell into his arms, crying from fear and release and joy. Tears stung his own eyes. "I thought I'd never find you," he said, smoothing her hair away from her eyes, his hands trembling.

"I knew you would," she said.

He helped her up the bank, taking off his jacket as they walked and putting it around her shoulders. "I'll build a fire—"

"Where's Andy?" she interrupted, her teeth clattering together.

"He's back at the wagon. I don't know what's wrong with him…"

"He just collapsed," she said. "We have to help him. His heart—"

"But we need to get you out of those wet clothes—"

"No time for that," she said. "They'll warm up as we ride. Let's go now. Hurry."

The urgency in her voice convinced him she was okay for the time being. Out of the water, the cuts and scrapes were beginning to bleed, but nothing looked terribly serious. He pulled a clean blue bandanna out of his pocket and pressed it against the worst cut, which was on her forehead. She took over applying pressure and he climbed atop Yukon, lowered a hand and helped her into the saddle to sit before him.

As it happened, they arrived back at the wagon just before the first cattle began to cross the river. They found Andy still out like a light, but his breathing was regular and his pulse strong. Between the two of them, they managed to get him into the back of the wagon where he rolled on top of all the bedrolls under the cover, never so much as opening an eye.

"At least he won't get trampled," Tyler said. He glanced at Julie who was beginning to show a little color in her face. "You need to put on dry clothes and it should be now rather than later.

"But Andy—"

"You change clothes and I'll go find Dr. Marquis and get him here to check things out, okay?"

"Yeah, that's a good idea."

He caught her chin and when she didn't pull away, lowered his head and kissed her. "I thought you were dead," he said.

"So did I."

They stared into each other's eyes until Andy snorted in his sleep, and then they both looked down at him. "He looks like he tied one on," Tyler said. "Like he's sleeping off an all-night boozer."

"All he drank was coffee," Julie said. "And that was out of his thermos."

"Could he have spiked it?"

"No, I would have smelled any alcohol in it."

They looked back at each other again, and then away and Tyler had the distinct feeling they'd both come to the same conclusion: Someone had drugged Andy's coffee.

"Where's the thermos now?" he asked, looking around.

"I don't know. I grabbed it when I was falling."

"Did it go over the side with you?"

"It must have. I just don't remember."

He pushed back his hat. "Well, it's gone now." And so was any potential evidence.

Chapter Ten

Dr. Marquis listened to the old guy's heart, thumbed up his eyelids and shined a light, felt his pulse. "Can't be certain," he said, trying to get comfortable in the cramped space, "but I see no indication of a heart attack or stroke. He just seems to be flat dead asleep."

"That's what we thought," Tyler said.

"Did he take a barbiturate or something?"

"I know he didn't take anything intentionally," Tyler said. "He knew his job was to get Julie safely across the river and he would never have jeopardized her welfare on purpose."

"Yet, people sometimes self-medicate without advertising it," Dr. Marquis mused. "You know, like with allergy medicine."

"Not Andy," Tyler insisted, "And never in a situation like this."

"He didn't know what was happening to him," Julie said, recalling his mumbled comments. She'd twisted her damp hair into a knot at the back of her neck and dressed in her warmest clothes, but she still had Tyler's sheepskin-lined jacket wrapped around her torso and belted to keep it tight.

"The amount of coffee that man drinks, you wouldn't think he had this kind of sleeping in him," the doctor said.

Tyler's brow furrowed. "You know about his habit?"

The doctor laughed, his hollow cheeks filling out a little. "The whole camp knows about his habit. Him and that thermos are inseparable. Maybe we should take a look at the contents—"

"It's gone," Julie said. "I'm afraid it went into the water when I did."

"I guess if there was something wrong with the coffee in general we'd all be sleeping or sick. Well, young lady, how about you?"

Julie shrugged. "I'm okay."

"Tyler told me what happened. That must have been terrifying. And it looks like that wound on your forehead needs cleaning and a good old bandage. If we were in the hospital, I might be tempted to take a stitch or two." He said all this while applying disinfectant to the gash on Julie's head. Next came a bandage. "Any other problems? Cuts? Contusions?"

"Nothing," she assured him.

"Hold out your hands," he said, and she did. He turned the palms upward. They were scratched and torn, and for a second she relived the frightening time in the water where she'd grabbed at anything she could reach in a desperate attempt to stop the relentless trip toward the rapids. She decided not to mention the huge bruises on her hip and shoulder where she'd hit against the rock that ended up being her salvation. There wasn't anything anyone could do about those.

"Really, I'm okay," she said.

"I could check you over…"

"No, no, please. I'm good. I need to get the wagon back on the trail. And Tyler, I know the way to the ravine, it's not far and it's mostly flat, so don't worry about me. Really, boys, I'm good."

She was aware that Tyler was staring at her as the doctor repacked his equipment and told her to let him know if she changed her mind.

That left Tyler and her standing next to the seat, high enough to look out over the herd which was slowly moving past them. It was easy to pick out the different guests as their shapes and postures were all unique. Meg Peterson, for instance, sat ramrod straight on her white horse, as alert as a squirrel. The secretaries were together, as usual, as were the fishermen brothers. John Smyth, while some distance away, sat in a saddle much as Tyler did, relaxed and yet watchful, seemingly at home—and once again familiar. Only this time she thought she finally figured out why.

Were one of these people drugging coffee, shooting arrows, planting spiders? It was hard to believe and yet the evidence seemed to be mounting. Tyler's hands landed on her arms. "Why are you frowning when you stare at John Smyth?" he asked.

She looked up at Tyler. "I didn't know I was."

He looked up. "Smyth must have felt your gaze. He's coming this way. Before he gets here, I want to make sure that you and I have a good talk this evening. I want you to go over everything that happened in Portland with me once again. The racketeering thing, Trill, your old boss, the bus, everything. We're running out of time. If someone drugged Andy's coffee we have to assume it was to put you in jeopardy, just like all the other incidents."

"I agree," she said, cold to the very core of her being.

"But there's something else, too. Your would-be killer has branched out to include a third party, namely Andy."

"I know. He could just have easily have fallen into the river as I did."

"Exactly. And drugged as he was, he would have drowned in a few seconds."

"Which means my continued presence on this trip could jeopardize the safety of more innocent people. I should leave at once." She looked at the trail on the other side of the river and thought about the long ride home....

"I wouldn't send you alone," he said.

"Tyler, how are you going to feed these people without my help?"

He shook his head.

"Let me get the wagon to the ravine. Even if you leave it there and somehow manage to take food with you for the remainder of the trip into the mountains, it would be better than leaving it here. I'll go back tomorrow. Maybe by then Andy will be himself again and he can come with me."

John Smyth arrived at that moment, bringing his horse to a stop by the wagon. His smiled greeting seemed forced. "Mele told me she needs you at the front of the line," he said, directing his comment to Tyler. His gaze then darted to Julie. "I might as well be honest with you, it's no secret something is going on. Is Andy all right?"

Tyler's voice was curt. "He will be."

For a minute, the three of them looked at each other in something resembling a stalemate. Tyler and Julie were both sitting now, and with John astride his horse, they were more or less eye to eye. Julie glanced from one man to the other; in some indefinable way, they were alike.

John cleared his throat. "It occurs to me you folks

might need help," he said softly, his voice barely audible over the sound of the nearby cattle. "What can I do?"

"Nothing," John said. "Thanks for asking, though."

"Can you help me harness the team?" Julie asked.

"Sure, I watched Andy a time or two."

"And then maybe you'd also consent to ride along with me?" Julie said, seeing a way to get Tyler back with the cows where he belonged.

"I'm happy to do whatever I can to help," John said, "but I have to warn you, I don't know how to drive a wagon—"

"Don't worry, I'll do the driving, you ride shotgun." Julie sneaked a peek at Tyler who looked like he was about to choke on something.

"I don't know," Tyler said.

"This will be fun," John interrupted. "I've always wanted to ride in a wagon."

Tyler leveled his gaze on John. "I'll be watching, you know, in case you need help."

"I think I can handle sitting all by myself," John said.

"That's not what I meant."

"Then what did you mean?" John said, a smile on his lips, but a challenge in his eyes.

Julie had never heard Tyler talk to a guest in this manner. Pushing amazement aside, she gripped Tyler's arm. "Mele needs you, remember? The wagon will be right ahead of the herd, you can come check on us anytime you want. No worries."

"Then it's settled," John said, and rode off toward the trees where the horses were tethered.

"I don't know, Julie," Tyler began. "Do you really want to be alone with that guy?"

"I have a feeling about him," she said.

"So do I."

"I think my feeling might be a little more positive than yours. Don't worry. Trust me," she added as her fingers trailed lightly down Tyler's sleeve to graze his hand. "And thank you for, well, saving me."

His answering gaze delved all the way to her heart. "Anytime."

"It's been quite a day so far, hasn't it?" John Smyth commented. He'd taken Tyler's directive very literally, his shotgun lying across his lap. Hopefully the safety was on.

"Yes," Julie said. Her hair was still wet but that didn't account for the chills that closed around her insides like a fist made of ice. Credit the nearby dense forest and the river that snaked within.

"I heard about what happened to you," he said, and glancing into the back, added, "and Andy. Weird."

"Very," she said. Hard not to wonder what the guests were thinking about this strange turn of events. It would have to be addressed that evening, like it or not. And then tomorrow, she would have to leave.

"Care to explain?" he added.

"It's a little complicated."

"I figured that."

She felt him staring at her and darted him a glance. "What?" she said.

"You and Tyler are in the middle of a divorce."

"How do you know that?"

"It doesn't matter how I know, I just do. I also know you left about a year ago. What I don't know is why you're back on the ranch."

"And why could that possibly matter to you?"

He chuckled. "You're a worthy adversary, Mrs. Hunt."

She didn't respond to that. "I have a question for you," she said.

"And if I answer it, will you confide in me? Will you tell me what really happened today and why you and Tyler were up most of last night?"

"You know about that?"

"Not everything, no."

"Did you see anyone else up and about?"

"Wandering around? No. Was there someone?"

"I think so."

"Ask me your question," he said.

She kept her eyes straight ahead on the trail, gazing over the broad golden backs of the team, aching for the time when the trail veered away from the trees and she would be able to see the countryside—and whoever might be lurking there with murder on their mind. Beside her, John cleared his throat.

She glanced at him and found his expression neutral. "The first day I was back on the ranch," she began, "I rode out to the creek. Tyler was already there, so I decided not to…bother…him. Then I realized someone else was watching him, too."

"Who?" John asked.

She shot him a quick look. "Do you really have to ask?"

"Ah," he said.

"You were really concentrating on him."

"Did you tell Tyler about this?"

"Not yet," she admitted. "I just figured out it was you a little while ago when I saw you sitting in your saddle at about the same distance and posture."

And as soon as she'd realized Tyler was the object of John's focus, she'd decided that because he didn't seem to be interested in her in a lethal way, maybe he could be trusted. "Whether I tell him depends on what you were up to," she added. "Or should I say, what you *are* up to."

"First just level with me. Why did you and Tyler split up?"

"That's none of your business."

"Was it because he has trouble sleeping or suffers from bad dreams or—"

"Absolutely not," she said. "Maybe you should explain why you think you know about us and why you lied about it."

"Don't you think you might have been alarmed if I'd revealed knowing your personal history?"

She assumed he wasn't after her, so he couldn't know how close to the mark his words hit. "I suppose I would have," she said.

"I just get the distinct impression Tyler is crazy about you."

She leveled a look at him. "Leave it alone, John."

He laughed softly. "All right, as you wish."

"So?"

"I didn't just come here for the cattle drive," he said after a long pause.

"I figured that part out."

He paused again, and Julie let him be. Who knew better than she that sometimes it took time to say things the right way? He finally sighed. "I'm going to have to ask you to keep this to yourself, at least for a while."

"I'm not making any promises," she said.

"I see. Well, just understand it's important for Tyler's well-being that he hears nothing about this until I'm sure I'm not making a mistake."

"Oh, for heaven's sake, John," she said, flicking him an impatient glance. "I wouldn't do anything to hurt Tyler."

"You left him, didn't you?"

"Okay, now you're skating on really thin ice."

He held up one hand. "This is me backing off. The fact is I think Tyler may be my half brother."

"What?" Julie looked at him again, this time for much longer, but the wagon bouncing through a series of ruts soon demanded her attention. The trail was finally leading away from the river and all those trees and they would soon start a slow climb toward Dead Man's Ravine. Right now, she would have preferred a less ominous-sounding destination.

"That's impossible," she said.

John had leaned back to check on Andy. "No, I don't think it is," he said, straightening up.

"Tyler is an only child." She glanced at him again and added, "Are you insinuating his mother or father had another child by a different relationship they never told him about?"

"No," John said. "I'm implying that Tyler may be adopted."

"But Rose—"

"Is a little on the defensive side, don't you think?" he interrupted.

"Not usually, but I have to admit she hasn't been herself since I got back."

"Which just so happens to be the same day I arrived and started asking her questions."

"Did you tell her what you just told me?"

"I didn't tell her anything." He took off his hat and ran a tanned hand through his hair. The sun was beating down hard and at these elevations, sunburn was always a worry, so Julie hoped he'd put it back on. But sitting there bareheaded, she fancied she saw a certain resemblance between John and Tyler. *No, that was impossible.*

He tugged his hat back on. "Listen," he said, "I don't want to hurt anyone. I don't want to disrupt lives if it isn't necessary. If this adoption had been on the up-and-up, I'd find a different away to approach things, but it wasn't. And, no, I'm not going to explain that right now. I may be totally wrong—"

"How long have you suspected this?"

"Not long."

"Do you have any kind of proof that Tyler is your half brother?"

"None that would stand up in court. I have hearsay and a tune."

"What do you mean a tune?"

"That melody Tyler whistles all the time. I'd forgotten it until I heard him, but as soon as I did, I recognized it from my own childhood. It's an old song from half a world away and the fact Tyler knows it is pretty suggestive."

"I think you're crazy," she said as the wagon once again swayed over uneven ground.

"Maybe I am, but there are no pictures of Tyler before the age of four in his mother's albums."

"There was a fire—"

"So she says. But where? There's no sign of anything ever burning down. In fact there's another house on the ranch, but it's really old."

"I know," she said. "Tyler and I used to live there."

"Well, neither that house nor the main lodge appears to have been involved in a fire."

"Rose told me a barn burned down decades before, destroying some mementos and pictures, things like that. Any trace of such a thing would be long gone by now."

He cocked an eyebrow. "I heard the same thing, but

really, who stores pictures of their small child in a barn, especially in Montana?"

"I don't know, John. This just sounds outlandish. Rose isn't a secretive person. I think if she and Tyler's father adopted a child, she would have been up-front about it."

"Maybe not if Tyler's biological father and mother were savagely murdered," he said.

"You'd better explain what you mean," she said.

"Not right now," he said quietly, his voice soft but hard as steel and it finally dawned on her that he was talking about his parents, whether or not they were Tyler's as well. "Do I have your word you won't say anything to him?" he added.

"Absolutely. And I beg you not to either." The road evened out enough where she felt secure letting Ned and Gertie find their way. Turning her full attention on John, she stared directly into his eyes. "Even if you find out it's the truth," she said, "think about what you're doing. Tyler is a Hunt, right down to the soles of his feet and those feet are firmly planted on the family ranch. I may be the kind who has to search for who I really am, inside I mean, but Tyler isn't. He knows who he is and where he belongs. So promise me you'll err on the side of caution when it comes to being truthful."

"I do give you my word," he said, "but you have to understand there's more at stake than you know."

She nodded and stared ahead again, sick in the pit of her stomach thinking about what this would do to Rose and Tyler if it was true. It would mean Tyler's childhood was built on lies.

"So, now it's your turn," he said, nodding toward the back of the wagon. "What happened to Rip van Winkle?"

"We think someone drugged his coffee."

"And you ended up in the river because…"

"Because he collapsed and I fell over the top of him when the horses took off."

"And the someone who did this to Andy—that person is really after you?"

She narrowed her eyes. "How do you know all this?"

"It's kind of what I do," he said.

"Which is?"

"I'm former police, former bodyguard, former detective. I know when someone is in trouble. And you, Julie Hunt, are in trouble, aren't you?"

His past careers coupled with his current goal explained a lot about John Smyth, such as why he was always asking questions, why he was always around. Maybe it wasn't wise, but she found herself trusting him. "Someone is trying to kill me," she said. "Someone on this cattle drive, I think."

"Why?"

"Good question."

"And you don't know the answer?"

"Well, I'll go out on a limb and say it's a certainty that I know something I shouldn't. I'm just not sure what it is."

"Ah," he said. "That makes perfect sense."

Chapter Eleven

Tyler was relieved to see Julie's tall, slender shape darting around the chuck wagon as he rode Yukon into camp. For a second, as he approached, he watched her, marveling at how energetic she appeared after the night they'd had to say nothing of her struggle in the river.

Funny, but he'd always thought of her as being fragile and delicate. The hard-working dynamo she'd morphed into was a continual surprise and bore little resemblance to the woman she'd been two or three years ago when she last went on one of the cattle drives with him.

She seemed to sense someone coming and looked up suddenly, her expression terrified for an instant until she apparently recognized him. He saw a flash of white teeth as he stopped the horse downwind of the wagon. "How's Andy?" he asked as he dismounted and dipped his hands into a pail of water. He found a sliver of soap with which to wash, then splashed some on his face as well. She handed him a towel.

"He's stirring a little now. Two of your wranglers set up a tent for him and carried him over there. I go check on him every once and a while just to make sure he's okay," she added as she poured him a mug of coffee. He must have looked a little leery of the cup, for she assured him she'd scrubbed it clean before making another pot, just in case.

He looked toward the bottom of the bluff where several tents had been taken from storage—apparently many of the guests had asked for tents tonight and Tyler wasn't surprised. People who chose to sleep under the stars when they were camping on grassy shores often chose the coziness of a roof over their head for a stark ravine. It was one of the reasons he'd chosen it as a campsite. Besides having food and water for the livestock for a night, it was rugged, different than the shores of the river which they'd experienced the night before, enriching the whole experience.

This camp also boasted a lean-to stocked with extra supplies. They'd found years before that spending a couple of days at the beginning and end of each season to stock the shacks with things like tents, some larger cooking gear and various sports equipment cut way back on the need to transport everything each and every time they made a trip. As out of the way as this camp was, it was also a favorite for ride-outs that didn't include a cattle drive.

"And how did it go with John Smyth?"

"Fine. I told him what really happened today."

He raised his eyebrows. "You did? That surprises me."

"Well, he mentioned a background in law enforcement and he was already figuring things out. Turns out he was a bodyguard at one time. I thought maybe we could use an extra set of eyes and ears."

He didn't like this development. He wasn't sure about Smyth. Looking around camp now, he saw very little movement. "Where is he?"

"After helping me drag the firebox out of the shack,

he joined some of the others for a hike to explore the stream that cuts through the bottom of the ravine. I think Nigel and Vincent convinced everyone there were fish in the stream."

"And those who didn't go fishing?"

"Dr. Marquis is taking a nap, and the Taylors are reading in their tent. Bobby Taylor went with the hikers."

He stared at her as she sliced onions. "So, we're alone."

"Trust me, I am constantly on the lookout. We're about as alone as you can get on a cattle drive."

He rested a hip against the wagon and pushed his hat back a little. "Tell me again what your boss said when you confessed you'd been spying on him."

She slid the pile of onions to one side of the cutting board and started cleaning green beans, one foot resting on an overturned crate. He grabbed a handful and helped her.

"Let's see. He was angry with me, which I expected—"

"No, what did he say about Trill?"

"That he didn't know him."

"Did he offer any explanation about the picture of himself taken with Trill and the other two men?"

"No. But, you know, he was at that conference to give a lecture and those are often followed by luncheons or dinners and many times, colleagues or even strangers eat a meal together without really knowing each other well, if at all. Trill might have been there investigating Professor Killigrew and arranged a picture."

"I know you've been busy trying to stay alive, but ask yourself this—why did your boss have a picture of strangers tucked into his private notebook?"

"I don't know. But he doodled and wrote in code. It was all pretty strange."

"Doodle?"

"Just geometric shapes. Triangles and rectangles."

"Back to the photograph. It was the only one in there, right?"

"Yes."

"So if Killigrew didn't know Trill, he must have known one of the other men. And you didn't recognize either one?"

As she pulled the string from a bean, she thought back to the photo. Killigrew with his mane of untamed white hair. Trill in a tan suit looking more like an insurance salesman than a cop. A third man of considerable weight with his back half-turned to the camera, and a smaller man, darker, round face, glasses, forty or so, in motion. "I don't think I'd ever seen either one of them before, but now in some indefinable way, they both seem familiar to me, as though I've thought about that photograph so often I've gotten to know them. That sounds crazy. What does all this mean?"

"I don't know what it means. But you've described Killigrew as quite aggressive when you talked to him."

"Who could blame him after what I did?"

"Hear me out," he said, snapping a bean in two. "Trill, whoever he really is, accused him of racketeering, correct?"

"That's right."

"Was he specific about what they suspected him of doing?"

"No. In fact he was very vague."

"As I understand it, racketeering is illegal business involving a group of people, like organized crime, for instance, rather than an individual. Did Trill mention any mob affiliations or anything like that?"

"None." She rubbed her eyes and shook her head. "He threw out a lot of words. Tax evasion and blackmail were mentioned. It was like they suspected the professor of being some horrible gangster. It didn't make any sense to me. That's why I was so sure they were barking up the wrong tree for the wrong man."

"And you said he was concerned about something that was going down this summer, too, right?"

"Yes. In a few days the professor has another one of those conference lectures to deliver. Trill wanted me to gather information and listen in on phone calls. I can't believe I went along with it. What kind of turncoat am I?"

He stared into her eyes. "I know you feel bad about what you did, Julie," he said. "But I want to suggest that there was some part of you that wondered about Killigrew, that maybe you harbored some suspicion that he isn't on the up-and-up. That may have been why you allowed yourself to get talked into this, so you could prove to yourself, and then to Trill, that Killigrew was as upstanding as you wanted him to be."

She looked angry for a moment and he thought maybe he'd stepped too close to the truth. Then she shook her head. "It was a dream job, Tyler. His assistant retired rather suddenly and he needed someone. It was the first job I interviewed for and he said I was perfect. At the time, I was desperate to have work and space—well, you know all about that. I jumped on it."

"Makes sense to me," he said, hating her choice of words. She'd been desperate to escape *him*. Desperate to make an income because she'd refused to take money from *him*. And that space she'd craved? Space away from *him.* A shot of pure anger burned in his stomach and he had to concentrate to make it go away.

"I'm going to try to get a hold of his former assistant when we get back to the ranch," she said. "I know her name is Marti Keizer and she retired on the coast south of Seaside, Oregon. How many people with that name can possibly be roaming around a small town?"

"That's a good idea. Had she worked for him long?"

"I guess just a couple of years. No one talked about her much, but that wasn't too odd because there were so few people in the office and everyone was kind of uptight and private. There was someone else before her, but I don't know who."

"Listen," he said after taking a deep breath. "I'm riding up on the ridge where the reception is better to try to call the ranch and make sure my mother isn't sicker than she let on. Come with me and call that friend of yours. See if anything is happening back in Portland you need to know about, including whether there's a hunt of some kind going on for you."

"I can't leave now. This is the last dinner I'll be here to cook. I'm leaving in the morning—"

"You've got a great start on dinner. I'll help you stow this stuff. We'll be gone only an hour or so. Leave a bowl of fruit out for anyone who's hungry."

She agreed and they quickly put things away in the cooler, then they both got on Yukon, this time Julie riding behind. He toyed around with going to saddle up Andy's horse for her, but in the end decided not to waste the time. The trail wasn't a hard one and Yukon had had a pretty easy day.

Also, it would be dishonest not to admit that he liked having Julie's arms around his waist, her head resting against his shoulder. He knew she wasn't asleep, but she was very quiet, and despite everything, the ride helped to dissipate his frustration.

He knew from experience cell phone reception would be adequate on top of this ridge. They got off Yukon who wandered a few feet away to nibble on a patch of grass and Julie stretched out on a sun-baked flat rock. "You go first," she called, closing her eyes, her face turned up to the sky.

For a moment he stared at her. Tomorrow, she and Andy would head back to camp and she'd be gone before he got home from this trip. He turned his back on her beautiful face and placed his call.

Heidi answered on the second ring and laughed when he asked to speak with his mother. "Rose is out on a ride with a group of bankers from Cincinnati," she said. "They were a sudden booking and she's sworn to make sure they have the time of their lives because she thinks they may come back again this fall."

"Is she feeling up to all that?"

"Apparently. She's been running around like crazy since you guys left."

"She was ill two days ago."

"I know."

"Did she go to the doctor?"

"No. She whitewashed the gazebo."

He felt the oddest sense of disconnect. What the hell? Bottom line: If his mother was up to riding a horse and painting a gazebo, she couldn't be on death's doorstep. He said goodbye to Heidi, clicked off the phone and turned back to Julie.

She was sitting up now, staring at him, those mysterious eyes of hers mesmerizing. "How is Rose?"

"Apparently she's fine," he said.

"Well, that's good news. Why do you look confused?"

"Because she's lying to me about something," he said.

It was impossible not to pick up the way Julie's gaze shifted and he had the sudden feeling she knew more than she was telling him and that it concerned Rose Hunt. "Do you know what's going on with her?" he said, hitching his hands on his waist.

She looked back at him. "I don't."

"Truthfully?"

"Truthfully."

He shook his head. "I'll figure it out later. Your turn." He handed her the phone and sat on the rock as she got to her feet and placed her call.

After several seconds he heard her say something in a voice that sounded like she was leaving a message on a machine. "She's still not answering," Julie said. "I'm calling her brother."

She had to call information for his number, but was soon connected. He heard her ask a question or two, then she bent her head and listened as she walked in little circles. At one point her head popped up and she looked straight at Tyler. The expression in her eyes shot him like a bullet. He got to his feet and walked toward her because it struck him she was close to collapsing.

She mumbled something into the phone and clicked it off, handing it back to him as though it might bite her.

"What is it, Julie?"

"Nora is dead," she said, staring up at him, her eyes huge. "Oh, my God, she was murdered two nights ago. The police think she interrupted a burglary."

"Two nights ago? Is that the night you called her from the ranch?"

"Yes. And Roger Trill was at my place when she got off the phone. She was going over there to pretend to see if she could tell if I took anything." Her lips trembled and tears flooded her eyes. She stepped away, resuming the pacing, her steps clumsy through her tears. "She called George to tell him she was going to be late getting to his place, but he said her voice sounded funny and she was going on about a suitcase or something. He wasn't sure what she was talking about. But she never showed up and he sent a friend to check on her and she'd been stabbed. What if she told Trill—"

"What if she did?" he said, clutching her arms to keep her from spinning off into space. "Why would he hurt her just because she spoke with you? She didn't even know exactly where you were."

"But if she mentioned the call, maybe he wanted her cell phone to try to trace me."

"He's a cop, Julie. I think he could subpoena her cell phone records."

"But that would mean he was being open with his department and that seems unlikely."

"Then he could have probably talked her out of it. You told me she was worried about you and that he'd fed that worry by making it sound as if you were damn-near suicidal. I bet she would have done whatever he asked. There would be little cause to hurt her."

She pulled an arm away and mopped her eyes with a sleeve. He handed her a bandanna and she blew her nose.

"Why did she tell her brother she was bringing a suitcase?" Tyler asked. "Was she going to stay with him?"

"I doubt it. His place is really small and there's a nurse who spends every night from around eleven o'clock until morning. There'd be nowhere for her to sleep. Besides, George sounded confused…" Julie's voice trailed off as another thought struck her.

"What is it?" Tyler demanded.

"What if Nora found a suitcase and clothes missing from my apartment?"

"But you said you didn't take anything."

"I didn't. But what if that's why Trill wanted her to come over to my place? What if he'd secretly taken things the first time he was there and now he wanted Nora to confirm stuff was missing to establish that I was truly gone of my own will. Only she knew I hadn't been home so she'd know he was trying to put something over on her. And what if he saw right through her pretense to believe whatever story he made up, so he killed her and made it look like a bad robbery?"

"That is one hell of a lot of what-ifs," Tyler said.

"I know." Her tears had stopped for a few minutes, but now they began again. "Poor George. I don't know what he's going to do without Nora. And Tyler, it's because of me, I just know it."

He reached out to hold and comfort her but he didn't say anything. There was nothing he could say that would help, mainly because he thought she was probably right.

SOMEHOW, JULIE MANAGED to pull it together long enough to cook dinner. One of the calves had gotten itself stuck in a deep ditch, so two of the wranglers had to leave to rescue it and a couple of guests went along to help. Therefore, it was a smaller group who came through the chow line.

Andy had finally staggered out of his tent earlier and asked for coffee. She'd served him up a big mug along with the leftover cobbler from the night before.

He'd eaten, thanked her, suffered a once-over from Dr. Marquis and gone back to his tent where she suspected he'd spend the rest of the night. His eyes had only barely been half-open, but he'd listened attentively when she explained that she was probably the reason he had been drugged.

Those who had gone after the calf returned in high spirits while Julie dished up hot peach crisp. It was her plan to get the dishes done as soon as possible so she could turn in early. Fatigue had come and gone and now she felt like one of the walking dead. If she was going to get Andy back to the ranch tomorrow and affect an escape from Montana for herself, she needed to be able to think clearly.

What she purposely avoided thinking about was Nora's death.

Tyler seemed to be waiting until everyone had finished downing a cocktail or two. She imagined he hoped a little alcohol would make his revelations go over easier.

He finally met Julie's gaze as he stood and tapped a fork against his tin mug. When he spoke, his voice carried over the whole camp. "Folks, please, may I have your attention," he began.

Every head turned his direction. Julie had the feeling they'd all been waiting for an explanation of the day's events that came from the source and not the rumor mill. "I want to tell you all that I'm sorry things were a little rough today and that there was so much hanging out by the river. You all deserve an explanation and to be made aware why there are going to be a few changes."

John Smyth stood up. "Excuse me for interrupting you," he said, "but we all know what happened. We've all talked about it and we all know Julie and Andy are planning on leaving tomorrow morning and frankly, it doesn't sit well with any of us. As a matter of fact, we've unanimously agreed that if she goes back, we'll all go back. We started this together and we want to finish it together."

"That's very nice," Tyler said, "But you don't understand the situation—"

"Actually, we do understand it," John said. "You have a herd to get to pasture and a woman in jeopardy."

Meg Peterson stood up, waving her hand. "We all understand," she said. "John and Dr. Marquis filled in some of the blanks for us. We know someone drugged Andy and has taken some deadly actions toward Julie. We won't hear of her and Andy going off on their own. There must be someone else out there intent on doing her harm. It simply can't be one of us."

Julie's tears were back, but they weren't the guilt-induced gut-wrenchers from a couple of hours before when she heard about Nora. These were grateful tears as she glanced from one face to another.

"Look at it this way," John said. "We're all watching out for her now. We're all keeping an eye on each other, too, and that's a good thing. She's safer here now that things are out in the open. If there's a stranger up to no good, one of us is bound to see him. If one of us isn't who they say they are, they are on alert that this is no longer a secret and they'd be well served to back down."

Tyler shook his head. "Sorry, folks, you don't know what you're volunteering for. I'm already taking chances I shouldn't take. This stunt today was the crowning glory. Any one of you could have been hurt by this culprit's ruthlessness. You're not aware of the full scope—"

"Are you talking about what happened to Julie's sleeping blanket?" John Smyth said.

"You know about that?"

"Not the details, no, but I know there was a problem and it kept you two up most of the night."

"And how about that arrow?" Bobby Taylor added, gesturing at the arrow still stuck in the side of the wagon. "Heck, we know someone narrowly missed hitting Julie with that thing."

Julie spoke into the ensuing silence. "I'm so sorry to have impacted your vacations in such a negative way."

"You mustn't worry about that," Meg Peterson said as the three secretaries rushed to Julie's side.

"We all voted, even the wranglers and cowboys," one of them said. "We all want to get the herd up to the meadow and we all want to stay together. In fact, you're sleeping with us tonight in our tent. So, don't cry."

"This will be like the Old West," Meg said.

"Yeah. All of us against the bad guys," Bobby added.

Julie tried to speak, but she just couldn't.

"And we're doing the dishes tonight," one of the other secretaries added. "You need to get some rest. I can't imagine how harrowing that river must have been."

"From now on, Julie, we're on a buddy system and you aren't ever going to be alone," John Smyth added.

THE SECRETARIES WERE as good as their word. Two of them stayed to wash dishes and the third—Sherry— went with Julie to their tent. Julie laid out her bedroll and opened it completely before getting inside, searching every inch with the flashlight for spiders or other miscreants. Thankfully, she didn't find a thing.

Julie had thought her eyes would close the moment her head hit the pillow, but oddly enough, she found sleep elusive. Dr. Marquis paid a visit by saying "knock, knock" outside the tent and entering when Sherry opened the flap.

"Tyler told me you had an upsetting telephone call today," he said, looking from her to Sherry. "I wondered if you'd like a sleeping aid."

"No," Julie said, sitting up. "Thanks, but I'll be fine and I'll need to be up early to get breakfast going."

"I'm going to help you," Sherry said.

Julie started to protest, then thought better of it. Who was she kidding? Company and an extra pair of hands would be great. "Thanks," she said instead. "I appreciate the offer."

"The drug won't knock you out," the doctor said. "All it will do is relax you so that you can sleep."

Again Julie shook her head. "Really, thank you, but I'll be fine."

"Well, you let me know if you change your mind," he said, and left.

Tyler was next and this time, Sherry explained she was going to stand outside the tent while they said goodnight.

"Obviously, everyone knows we're married," Julie said as the flap closed behind the secretary.

"Everyone knows everything," Tyler said, but there was a smile in his eyes as he knelt down to perch on his heels beside her.

"I'm sorry about the mutiny on my behalf," Julie said. "I could sneak away—"

"No, you couldn't. John organized a camp watch. People are taking shifts, two at a time, I might add, keeping an eye on things and each other."

"I can't imagine the guests are finding this situation

very enjoyable. Aren't they worried they could be cavorting with a killer?"

"I don't think so," he said, reaching out to smooth a piece of hair away from her eyes. How she wanted him to slide into the bed with her, just to hold her, just to take away some of the pain. How selfish was that?

"You need sleep," he said. "Good night, Julie." He leaned over and kissed her forehead.

"If it's not time for your shift with the herd, maybe you could stay for just a minute?" she asked softly.

He wrapped his big hand around her smaller one. "I can be a few minutes late," he said. "Lay down."

She did as he directed.

"Are you warm enough?" he asked, tucking the bedding up around her chin.

She nodded.

He hummed a few bars of the song he usually whistled, a tune she always associated with him, a tune she'd always found comforting. But this time she thought of the bomb John Smyth was waiting to drop on Tyler and her stomach clenched.

Chapter Twelve

Tyler awoke near daybreak out near the herd where he'd thrown his bedroll after his turn at watch. His thoughts immediately jumped to Julie and he rolled up his bed and slung it under an arm before he was fully awake.

Once again the scene that greeted his eyes as he approached camp was infinitely reassuring. Not only was Julie hard at work making breakfast, but two of the Wall Street secretaries were helping her. John Smyth was up as well, flipping pancakes. Even Andy was there, seated on a rock, his mug in his hand. Apparently bad coffee the day before hadn't turned him off the stuff.

Tyler didn't know what his mother's issue was with John, but he'd decided she was wrong about him. Julie trusted him and he'd come through for her. For that matter, he'd come through for the whole group. Many of the wranglers were like Mele—young, relatively inexperienced, especially with violence, more trained in serving people than keeping an eye on them. Tyler decided he'd go along with Julie's instincts and trust John—up to a point.

Within a couple of hours, the chuck wagon was ready to leave camp, Julie taking the reins, Dr. Marquis riding shotgun beside her, his horse tethered to the back. Andy would ride alongside them.

"Had that thermos for twenty-eight years," Andy grumbled as he and Tyler hitched up the team. "Like to get my hands on whoever messed with it."

"Do you have any ideas?" Tyler asked as he nudged Gertie into her harness.

"None. I left it in my saddle bag. Anyone could have doctored it."

"That's what I figured," Tyler said.

"And I was just getting it broke in proper like," he added.

"Tell you what," Tyler said, fastening the last buckle. "Get one of those fancy kind that actually holds heat and it's on me."

"You're on," Andy said. "But what do I do for coffee today?"

Tyler shook his head as he watched Andy ride toward the chuck wagon which soon took off, Julie at the reins, Dr. Marquis seated beside her, Andy bringing up the rear.

The rest of them gathered the strays, and two hours later, took off trailing the wagon. As always, the cattle instinctively found the easiest route while humans worked to keep them more or less together. It was a lot more efficient to keep an animal from straying than rounding them up once they headed off on their own.

Tyler hadn't ridden this far afield yet this year and he was surprised to find several minor rock slides. He warned the wranglers to keep an extra eye on the poorer riders in the group and was glad the doctor was safely seated in the wagon up ahead.

Was one of them a killer? He couldn't quite buy the theory of a stranger following along behind, drugging Andy's thermos when he wasn't looking, trying over and over again to harm Julie without succeeding.

If the goal was to kill her, then shoot her, already, and get it over with. That meant the goal wasn't to kill her. But wait…if the goal was simply to scare her or harm her, then why not be more overt? To Tyler, everything pointed toward someone trying to make what happened to Julie look like an accident. A fatal accident.

What would that person do now that the whole camp knew something was afoot? Suddenly, his allowing the guests to override his common sense seemed like a really stupid idea and as they reached the top of the hillside, he came to a conclusion. He would send half the wranglers on ahead with the cattle and half of them back with the guests before something terrible happened. All they needed was a liability suit brought about by injury, or heaven forbid, death. Talk about destroying the ranch…

Decision made, it was all he could do to keep going forward, but there were just a couple more hours to go before they made camp and people were too spread out to effect any changes right that minute anyway.

He tried to do something of a head count. He could see the secretaries trying to steer a group of about six heifers and their calves with the help of Bobby Taylor and Mele. John Smyth wasn't far away, riding near the two fishermen brothers. The older Taylors were taking care of the cliffside flank like seasoned pros.

Tyler looked around for Meg Peterson who usually rode with the secretaries, but not today. Too many terrible things had happened not to grow alarmed at her absence, and he pulled Yukon to a stop, turning in his saddle and shading his eyes to look behind him. A glimpse of white announced her horse's presence, out near the rim of the trail next to a precipitous drop of fallen rocks that cascaded down the hillside. Meg was in the saddle, but although she wasn't a bad horse-woman, he didn't want her that close to the unstable edge of the trail.

"Come on, boy," he urged Yukon and started the ride back to her, wishing he could shout out a warning but not wanting to take a chance of spooking a cow—or a guest.

It appeared she was taking photos with a handheld camera. Perhaps she sensed his focus on her. Her head went up. Her hat was pushed far back on her sunburned face, but she was too far away and the sun was too high in the sky for Tyler to make out her expression.

She waved an arm as though to greet him. Her horse reared back a little, dancing near the border of the bank. All Tyler could think was that the combination of an overconfident rider and a startled horse was never good. Sure enough, Snowflake took off.

Meg was obviously pulling back on the reins but it was doing little good. Tyler watched the scene unfold with cruel clarity as all four of the animal's feet slid over the side of the trail and started down the crumbling shale. Meg sat far back in the saddle, instinctively using her body as a counterweight to the horse's forward momentum as a small avalanche of dirt and stones formed a brown cloud around them.

The whole episode was oddly quiet, the only sounds being the crumbling rock. Meg appeared to be too startled to cry out and the horse was obviously fighting for her life. Tyler rode hard, wondering what in the world he could do to help.

He threw himself off Yukon a few feet from the compromised edge, dropping the reins in haste. As he looked over the side, he saw the horse lose her battle and fall forward onto her knees. Meg immediately flew right over the top of the horse's head, her body landing several feet farther down with a horrible thud. Snowflake was up again almost at once, and this time she found footing, taking her parallel with the face of the slope and galloped away in a cloud of dust.

Meg Peterson lay on a narrow shelf of land about twenty feet down the slope. Tyler heard horses approaching and turned to find John Smyth had joined him. In the distance, he could see some of the wranglers headed back his way.

Narrowing his eyes, he peered down at Meg's still body again, taking his first real breath when he detected the rise and fall of her chest and a movement of her legs.

"Did she make it?" John asked, grabbing his lasso off his saddle.

"So far. We've got to get her off that ledge before she accidentally rolls off." Tyler grabbed his lasso, too, and started tying a square knot to unite the two. They needed at least one more lasso, though.

"Do you want me to go after her horse?" John asked.

"No, I need you here to help me. Get one of the others to go. It'll probably head back to the canyon where we spent the night. And send someone up ahead to get the doctor. Tell whoever goes to trade places with him and help Julie get the wagon back here as fast as she can. Damn, she's probably already at the camp."

Wranglers and guests alike began arriving to see what was wrong and offer help. Another lasso was donated and another knot secured, then Tyler tied a bow knot and slipped the loop over his own head down to his waist. It was a gesture eerily reminiscent of the one Julie had done the day before when she was stuck in the middle of the river.

"I'm going down to make sure she can be moved,"

Tyler said, looking from face to face, landing last on John's. He would be hard-pressed to say why he trusted this man even if he had time to try to figure it out.

"There aren't any trees to wrap the line around for leverage, so playing out the line is going to fall directly on you guys," he added, and amid a chorus of encouragement, stepped backward off the rim of the trail. His boots immediately slid on the rocks and he started to fall. The rope yanked up under his arms. As the men on top adjusted their hold, he did the same and when he began repelling again, it was slower and at an angle.

Within a few minutes, he'd landed on the shelf and was kneeling beside Meg, whose crumbled glasses lay broken beside her in two pieces. Her eyes were open and dazed.

"I'm mighty glad to see you," she said.

He hoped his smile was reassuring. "Can you sit up? Is anything broken?"

"I don't know. Maybe my wrist."

"Try sitting," Tyler said. He wasn't feeling real secure about this ledge. It seemed his added weight had created additional erosion and the sound of skittering rocks was a constant.

He helped her sit, cautioning her to take it slow. She'd landed on her hands and they were bleeding as was a cut or two on her face. She looked up at him, tears in her eyes. "This really hurts," she said, cradling her right hand with her left. "I think it's broken."

"May I look?"

"Don't touch it, though," she screamed as his fingers landed lightly on her good hand.

"I won't."

She unfolded her left fingers to reveal the injured

hand. The blood on her skin seemed to come from contusions and not bones poking through the skin.

"At least it's not a compound break," he said.

She clutched it to her breast. "Is the doctor up there waiting for me?"

"He will be soon," Tyler assured her. "I sent someone as soon as you fell." While he spoke, he took the rope from around his waist and slipped it back over his head. Somehow this woman was going to have to get up the slope with just one hand to help steady herself. All the medical supplies were on the wagon.

He slipped the rope over her head, careful not to hit her hand. Then he took off his vest and helped her button it with her injured arm tucked inside. It wasn't real tight on her even with one arm pinned against her torso, but he adjusted it as well as he could so at least the hand wouldn't flap around as she the men above pulled her to safety.

"Can't we call for a helicopter?" she asked, clearly unimpressed with the rope.

"The telephones don't work very well out here," he said. We'll get you back where it's safe and if the doctor thinks you need to be airlifted, I'll ride to the top of the plateau and call for help."

"This all seems so old-fashioned," she said, looking up at him as he finished securing the rope. "Is your wife responsible for what happened to me?"

"You mean your fall?" he asked, surprised when she nodded. "Why would you think that? What exactly happened anyway? Why did Snowflake go over the side that way?"

"I don't know," she said. "I dropped behind to get a few pictures. The horse just seemed to get a wild hair as though something spooked her. Next thing I knew, she'd started down that slope. Did something frighten her? Did whoever is behind all these shenanigans mistake me for Julie?"

He glanced down at her short, plump form and sunburned face. No two women looked less alike than Meg Peterson and Julie Hunt. "I don't see how that's possible," he said.

"I don't see how you can discount what happened to me," she said. "By trying to save her, we put ourselves in jeopardy and you let us."

He wasn't going to stand there and argue with a frightened, injured guest who was obviously in pain especially when he suspected she could be right. "Let's just get you up top so the doctor can set that wrist."

"I want to go home," she said. "It's dangerous out here and it's not any fun anymore."

"Yes, ma'am, it is dangerous," he said as he double-checked the knots. It was one reason everyone had to sign a waiver. This was a real cattle drive fraught with real danger on occasion, but he wasn't going to argue that either. The fact was he agreed with her, he was partially responsible for this no matter what its cause. He looked up the cliff and hollered. "John? Meg has what appears to be a broken wrist. She's not going to be able to help you hoist her much. Are you guys ready?"

"Ready," John's voice rang out.

"Just hang on to the rope with your good hand," he told Meg.

She nodded, then violently shook her head. "I can't do it," she said, looking up at the rocks and dirt and then down toward the trail far below.

"You have to," he said.

"Call someone, please," she said, fumbling in her pocket with her good hand. "Get a helicopter or a rescue team or something." The pitch of her voice climbed as she spoke—it sounded as though hysteria wasn't far behind.

He thought they'd already been over that, but she seemed close to hysteria. He took her phone and clicked it on. Nothing happened. "Your battery is dead," he said, handing it back.

She swore softly. "You must have one. Use it."

He took his phone from his pocket and turned it on, and showed her the face. "No signal."

As she grabbed for it, the phone slipped from his hand, bouncing against the cliff as it tumbled down the hill. Meg cried out in alarm and covered her eyes with her good hand. "I'm sorry, I'm sorry," she sobbed. "Oh dear, now what?"

"Don't worry about the phone. We're on our own, but you shouldn't worry. We're used to taking care of things ourselves. You're going to be fine."

"Maybe someone up there—"

"Not with these mountains all around us. Let me help you get back to safety."

"I just can't go up that little rope," she said, wiping at her tears. "What if they drop me?"

"Ma'am, we're wasting time. Come on."

"What about you?"

"They'll send the rope back down for me once you're safe. Now, pardon my hands, but I'm going to hold on to you while you get started."

Right on cue, the rope became taut again. "Keep it down around your butt or waist," he cautioned, and lifting and steadying her, helped her get her feet in position.

She was a lot smaller than he was and it still took the guys forever to get her to the top because she kept yelling at them to go slower. At last she disappeared from his view. He listened for the doctor's voice, but all he heard was a small cry from Meg.

"Everything okay?" he called.

The answer was the rope which trailed down the hill, the last five feet or so landing at his feet as he dodged the small shower of rocks that came with it. He hitched the rope around his own waist and yanked it to signal he was ready.

The climb up was tricky but accomplished without mishap. A couple of the wranglers caught him under the arms and helped him up the last foot or two.

He immediately looked to the welfare of his guest, expecting to see the doctor bending over her. But a tearful Meg Peterson stood in a circle of concerned wranglers and other guests, Red Sanders urging her to take a restorative sip from his hip flask.

"Where is the doctor?" Meg demanded.

Tyler looked past the herd toward the trail.

"Mele went after him over an hour ago," John said, his voice lowered.

Tyler's gut seized. A rider with Mele's skill should have caught up with the wagon in a hurry. Even given the fact the doctor was a poor horseman, there should be some sign of his return by now. Was Meg right? Did Snowflake's odd behavior and Meg's subsequent fall have something to do with the continued attacks on Julie? He barked orders at the wranglers as he mounted Yukon. John got on his horse, too.

"Where do you think you're going?" Tyler asked.

"With you. Objections?"

"No."

Once they cleared the herd of milling cattle, they rode as hard as Tyler ever had. He kept expecting to see a cloud of dust announcing an approaching rider, but time ticked by with no sign of anyone.

His great hope was that Julie and the doctor had reached the campsite and maybe the doctor had wandered off to look at the rocks or something and Mele was having a hard time finding him. That hope was dashed when they climbed over a rise only to finally see the chuck wagon in the distance, its tall stern facing them, the canvas cover billowing in the breeze. It looked as though the wagon had stopped in the middle of the trail next to an outcropping of huge boulders. The horses were still harnessed, but he could see no sign of movement.

Tyler pulled Yukon to a halt and took a minute to dig the binoculars out of his saddle bag. The whole thing struck him as a setup of some kind and he knew there was no good to come from riding into a trap.

John pulled his horse to a stop nearby. "See anything?" he asked.

Tyler peered through the glasses. "Mele is hovering over someone or something on the far side of the wagon," he said, heart in his throat. Was it Julie?

"Can you see anyone else?"

"No one. Andy's horse is gone, too." Maybe Julie was inside, under the cover....

He jammed the binoculars back in the case and gave Yukon his head. He knew the big bay would head for Gertie and Ned.

Within a few minutes, they were riding up to the wagon. Once again Tyler all but threw himself to the ground. He could sense John right behind him as they were both drawn forward by the frantic quality of Mele's voice.

"Over here," she called. "Thank God you came. Hurry, I think he's dying."

They found her on her knees. Andy lay on the ground in front of her and she was holding a blood-soaked cloth against his chest. His face was as chalky white as September dust.

"I was afraid to leave him to come for help," she said, looking up at them with anxious eyes.

John immediately knelt beside her. "I've had some training," he said. "Let me take over."

Tyler climbed into the wagon as Mele moved her hands. "Where are Julie and the doctor?" he asked right before he saw a puddle of blood on the seat. Under the seat was Dr. Marquis' medical bag, but it had taken at least one of the bullets and the contents were now broken and leaking. Tyler took the ranch medical kit out from under the wagon cover and handed it down to Mele, his stomach rolling like the ocean.

"I don't know," she said.

"What do you mean you don't know?"

She opened the kit and the bag next to John and Andy. As she handed John what he asked for, she looked up at Tyler. "Andy was like this when I got here. The horses were gone. I assume the doctor and Julie were taken by force. Andy's gun is on the ground beside him."

"He must have tried to defend them," Tyler said as he climbed down. He checked Andy's gun and found two rounds missing. Had Julie or the doctor taken the other bullet? Andy might have used the rifle, too, the one he carried on his horse. As Shasta was also missing.

Next he searched the ground, looking for some indication of how many horses may have been involved, but the ground was a mess of tracks. He walked a wider circle and found a few headed off to the east. He followed them a few steps, half afraid he'd find Julie's or Dr. Marquis's lifeless body discarded behind the rocks.

Hoping for a better view of the land off to the east, he climbed the outcropping, arriving at the top out of breath from exertion and anxiety. But the countryside that greeted his gaze was hilly and rocky, dotted with trees and seemingly devoid of any life.

He climbed back down. "I have to go after them," he announced as he grabbed Yukon's reins. "Who knows how much of a head start they have."

"At least two hours," Mele said. "Maybe as much as four."

"Listen, you two," he said, climbing back in the saddle. "Do what you can for poor Andy, then get him into the wagon and head back to the others. Mele, tell half the wranglers to take the cattle up to the pasture by themselves. John, you and the other half of the wranglers head back to the ranch with what's left of the guests."

"I'll come with you," John said, looking from the wounded man to Tyler's face. "Who knows what you're getting into."

Tyler shook his head. "Meg Peterson is going to be frantic when she learns the doctor isn't there to help her. She'll need you to stabilize her wrist and you've built a rapport with the others. Everyone is going to be very upset."

"Do you even know what direction they went?"

"Two or three sets of tracks lead off to the east, at least for a ways. Don't worry about me, just make sure the herd gets up to the meadow tomorrow and the guests start back today. And be careful. Whoever did this now has two hostages."

"You're the one who should be careful," Mele said, her eyes flooded with anxiety. "Who would do this? Why?"

Tyler shook his head again.

John stood up. "We'll start back to help you after we make sure—"

"No, don't. Who knows where tracking them will lead me? By the time you get back, I could be anywhere and I have a feeling it will be way too late for anyone to help."

John turned his attention back to his patient, but Tyler could see it was killing him not to ride along. Maybe all those years in law enforcement made sitting on the sidelines hard work.

Turning Yukon toward the east, he headed into the least hospitable countryside this area had to offer, full of rocks and canyons. Night was fast approaching. Who knew what he would find.

Julie. She was out there somewhere and he had to save her. That was all he needed to know.

Chapter Thirteen

Tyler was the first to admit he wasn't the best tracker in the world, and as the daylight faded and mile after mile passed with few clues to go on, he worried that he might have missed something. As his gaze darted between the horizon and the ground, he tried to figure out what had happened back at the wagon.

The blood on the seat probably belonged to Julie or Dr. Marquis. He didn't think it was Andy's for the simple reason Andy had probably been riding Shasta. Had they been ambushed? Someone could have easily hidden in those rocks, picked off Andy and jumped out. Julie would have been driving and Dr. Marquis was no doubt as lousy a shot as he was an archer or horseman. But maybe he tried to protect Julie and was shot for his efforts.

Tyler wouldn't allow himself to consider the thought that either one of them was dead. Surely he would have come across their bodies or seen vultures circling overhead.

He should have gone with Julie instead of riding with the herd. The switchback was tricky, and he'd always been careful to bring up the rear on that part of the trail. Today he'd been there to help Meg Peterson, but he hadn't been around to help Andy, Rob Marquis or Julie.

Common sense said if he'd been there, he'd be the one bleeding to death in the middle of the trail, but common sense tended to take a hike when so many things were going wrong.

Night was quickly approaching and Tyler was uncertain what to do. If he traveled in the dark he stood the chance of missing some sign of a detour. There was nothing out here. Why would anyone keep going in this direction with two unwilling hostages?

He finally stopped out of consideration for Yukon and the failing light. He wasn't going to start a fire, but perhaps the kidnappers would. Waiting until dark, he scrambled to the top of another crop of boulders and settled down to wait, his binoculars ready, his flashlight off. Unfortunately, he saw no sign of a distant fire or anything else that would pinpoint their location.

Digging for his flashlight, he had discovered the lunch he'd never gotten around to in his saddle bag and he started eating it, saving the apple for Yukon. It wasn't until he had almost finished the sandwich that he realized Julie must have made it that morning.

Peanut butter—his favorite, made by *his* wife. He swallowed the sudden lump and stared up at the stars, wondering if she was nearby doing the same, knowing she must be terrified....

And knowing, too, that if she had to go off and live without him, he was going to have to let her. Not just physically, but emotionally, for both their sakes. He had to let her go. Finding her alive was going to have to be enough for him. Her freedom to live her life was going to have to be enough. Anything but burying her, anything but that.

He was up and going at first light after a miserable night spent sleeping on the ground. He was cold, tired, worried sick. Two hours later he came across the first sign that he was heading in the right direction and he would have missed that if Yukon hadn't lowered his head and whinnied, snuffling the rocky earth.

By the time he dismounted, the horse was just finishing eating something crunchy. Tyler thought he detected a whiff of apple and wondered if the horse had found a discarded apple core. He looked around and caught sight of the sun reflecting off something else a few feet away. That turned out to be a foil-wrapped sandwich with a single bite taken out of it. Peanut butter and jelly...

"Thank you, litterbug, whoever you are," he grumbled and got back on Yukon.

No way to tell if the food had been eaten today or the day before, but he was reenergized by the fact he had proof they'd at least come this way. He had a feeling he was getting closer, a feeling prompted by nothing unless it was instinct.

The sun climbed in the sky and he rode. He had a canteen for a little water for himself, but it was dry out here and the horse must be getting pretty darn thirsty. As distances went and the crow flies, they were probably less that twenty miles from the meadow and forty from the ranch. In a car, it would be a hop, skip and a jump. On a horse, it just took longer.

He knew John would alert the police as soon as he got back to the ranch or call them if someone on the drive had a phone that would get a signal. Tyler half expected to see the helicopter Meg had wished for buzzing in from the south. But the skies were open, dotted with nothing more than wispy white clouds. It was getting warmer by the second.

At last, scanning with his binoculars, he spied movement off to the north. His heart about jumped in his throat. He focused in until he made out Shasta and a big roan—Marquis's horse, Tex. There was no sign of a human being. The horses weren't together. In fact, they seemed to be loose, both nibbling on the sparse grass, saddled, riderless, untethered, their reins dragging on the ground.

His heart sank as he lowered the glasses. There was absolutely no sign of Julie or the doctor or anyone else for that matter.

He urged Yukon forward, eyes peeled, gun at the ready, the image of Andy's wounded body fresh in his mind. Shasta and Tex sensed his approach and lifted their heads, neighing a greeting to Yukon. Shasta trotted toward them while the roan went back to grazing.

Try as he might, Tyler could see no sign of any human, not even a body. But the horses were loose and who knew how far they'd wandered since losing their riders?

He directed Yukon toward a pile of rocks that might afford him a little height. He had to find Julie; she had to be nearby.

The rocks were hot in the midday sun. Carrying his binoculars, he leaped from one boulder to another, climbing steadily toward the top, avoiding the inevitable crevices. When he reached the top, he glimpsed something blue halfway down the other side and instantly thought of Julie's faded denim shirt. This time his leaps were wild as he raced toward the blue, stopping abruptly when he saw that it was a shirt, but not Julie's.

Dr. Marquis lay partially in a crevice, his arm flung wide, a rifle on the rocks beside him. There was a make-shift bandage on his upper arm and it was covered with dried blood. Tyler knew he was dead the minute he saw him, but he still knelt to feel for a pulse, wondering what had killed the man, what he was doing on these rocks, and most of all, where Julie could be.

He heard a distinctive noise and jumped backward, almost falling as he skittered away from a sound no one who had ever heard it ever forgot.

Rattlesnake.

Even as Tyler watched, a baby snake slithered out from under Rob's thin body and across the rock in the opposite direction, stopping to coil as it sensed his presence. Another one appeared in another crevice and another one from near Tyler's feet. He jumped back so fast he almost fell off the rocks. He knew rattlesnakes were born live, independent, pugnacious and poisonous from the get-go. But they weren't born with rattles and he'd heard that unmistakable sound—the mother must still be around....

What was a rattler doing having babies this early in the season? He grabbed for the abandoned rifle and circled back to Yukon in a hurry. Where was Julie?

Shasta whinnied again as he got closer. He reached out to take her reins, but she tossed her head and trotted away from him.

"Shasta," he called, pulling Yukon to a stop. He needed to get out the binoculars and look for Julie, but he wasn't going back up on those rocks.

Shasta kept walking and he saw she had headed toward a small copse of stunted trees. Could the horse actually know where Julie was? He sped up and trotted past Andy's horse, arriving within a few minutes.

At first he didn't see anything, and then he picked out a dusty, white, rectangular shape lying under the trees, its surface covered with branches and leaves as though someone had sought to obscure it by kicking debris over the top. He recognized it as one of the Hunt ranch bedrolls fully extended, zipped from head to foot. It was absolutely still and yet there was the distinct shape of a human form under the canvas cover.

He had the gut-wrenching feeling he'd just found Julie and that he was too late. He bombarded his way through the trees, arriving beside the bag without taking a single breath. He fell to his knees and brushed off the cover, then unzipped it and folded it back, knowing what he would find and dreading the moment her sightless gaze met his.

Her appearance stunned him. Damp from perspiration, hair stuck to her face and neck, she was blindfolded with her own bandanna, gagged, wrists and ankles bound with rope. But she was alive. He could see the pulse beating in her throat and the way she recoiled when he touched her.

"Julie," he said, his voice barely a whisper.

Her whole body jerked and then she lay very still. He untied the blindfold and she looked up at him, fear in her eyes turning to tears as he removed the gag. She was sobbing by the time he hacked through the rope binding her hands and feet, and then she threw herself into his arms.

He held her trembling body as close as he could, amazed she was alive. "Are you hurt?" he asked, holding the sides of her face and staring at her.

She shook her head. "I'm so glad you're here—" she began but he didn't wait for her to finish. In that instant he forgot his vow to himself, to let her go, and when he claimed her lips it was as her husband, the man who loved her and needed her.

She tasted as sweet as she always did, and the desperation in her kisses instantly hiked up his libido. He wanted to possess her, right that moment and forever....

She broke away but clung to him as though he was a life preserver. "We have to get out of here," she whispered frantically against his neck. "Now, before he comes back."

"Before who comes back?" Tyler asked, looking beyond her to the three horses who by their calm demeanor suggested no one new was approaching. "Julie, who is behind all this?"

"Trill," she said icily.

"He's here?"

"No, his partner was. Dr. Marquis," she added, standing. "Only he isn't really a doctor."

Tyler stared at her for a moment, her words not making any sense to him. The man had bandaged wounds and listened to heartbeats. And yet, had he done anything any media-savvy adult hadn't read about or seen performed on a screen a hundred times?

"I finally recognized him," she added. "He was one of the men in the photograph I found in Professor Killigrew's notebook. The heavy-set one."

"But he's as thin as a rail," Tyler said as he got to his feet.

"He told me several days ago that he had his stomach stapled. I bet he isn't half the size he used to be. But none of this matters right now," she added, pulling on Tyler's sleeve. "He said he was going to find someplace his phone would get reception. You have a gun with you, we have to go someplace and hide and ambush him when he comes back for me—"

"He's not coming back," Tyler said. "He's dead."

Her eyes were very wide as she gasped. "Did you—"

"No, I didn't kill him. It appears he fell into a crevice

and landed in a nest of rattlesnakes. Who was he going to call? Did he say?"

"It must have been Trill. That's who sent him, who else? He was really mad that things hadn't turned out the way he planned. All those 'accidents' were meant to disable me so I would be unconscious and under a 'doctor's' care. He had a vial of something that would have stopped my heart had I survived any of the so-called accidents he arranged. He even tried to give me a shot last night, claiming it was a sedative. His goal was to make it look as though I died while he was trying to save me."

"What about things like autopsies and the fact the real Dr. Marquis will show up eventually? Sooner or later, your death would be known for what it really was—murder."

"He killed the real Dr. Marquis," she said. "He bragged about it." She wrapped her hands around her arms as though she was cold.

"Let's get you out in the sunlight," he said although he was hot even standing under the trees.

"He said he was keeping me alive in case you caught up and he needed a bargaining tool," she said as they made their way through the broken branches, the bedroll now tossed over Tyler's shoulder. "His plan was to smother me after he knew he was safe."

"The real doctor made his reservation months ago. How could this guy have known about that?"

"I don't know. He just said he killed the doctor after the poor man landed at the airport. That's why you got that call saying he was held up in Chicago."

"He must have had a contact on the ranch," Tyler said with a sickening thud in his gut. "One of us. It's the only way he could have known the identity of one of our guests." None of this made sense.

"Does it matter right now?" Julie said as they stepped out from under the trees.

"I guess not right this minute. We have no way of knowing if your abductor completed his call before he died. He might have arranged a rescue. I think we'd better get out of here."

"We could check his phone," Julie said, rubbing her arms.

"No, we can't do that, not with the rattlers in the rocks. Let's just get away from here. It's going to be dark in a few hours."

She nodded but it was accompanied by a hasty look around.

"I don't have anything to give you to eat, but I do have water," he added as he fetched the canteen from Yukon's saddle.

Leaving her to drink, Tyler tied the bedroll to the back of Shasta's saddle, then quickly gathered the roan. He helped Julie mount Shasta, and the two of them took off the direction Tyler had come, trailing the roan behind.

"Why didn't he just shoot you?" Tyler asked. "Why threaten to smother you?"

She glanced at him and away. "I convinced him you were hot on his trail and that a shot would carry up here in these hills for miles and miles. I told him if he shot me, you'd know where he was and you wouldn't stop until he was dead."

She flashed him another look as though gauging his reaction to such bold declarations of what she meant to him. Her eyes were as much a mystery as ever. Did she have any idea how close to the truth her threats were? He doubted it.

"I just wanted to scare him into keeping me alive," she said softly.

"WHAT HAPPENED YESTERDAY?" Tyler asked as they rode. "You know, at the wagon."

Julie glanced over at him. "Oh, my God—Andy. How is he?"

"Not good. I left him with John Smyth and Mele. They were trying to get him stabilized before putting him in the wagon and taking him back to the ranch. What happened?"

"We were just riding along when all of a sudden the fake doctor produced a pistol I didn't know he had and shot Andy in the back. Andy fell off his horse, but he got a shot off first. I got conked on the head. When I woke up, he'd tied me up and thrown me over Shasta's saddle and I didn't know where we were. He was furious that he'd been forced into a direct confrontation. He said it was supposed to look like an accident and he probably wouldn't get all the money that was due him and it was my fault."

"And you're sure he was the man in the photo?"

"Yes. I asked him about Trill when he took the gag out of my mouth and he gave me that creepy smile he had. I told him I'd seen him in a photograph with Trill."

"So you think Trill hired him?"

"Yes. I think this guy and Trill were targeting Professor Killigrew, although I don't know why. But the professor must be in terrible danger and there's no way around the fact that I'm complicit. It must have something to do with his Seattle trip because that's what Trill was always asking about. I've got to warn Killigrew."

"As soon as we get back to the ranch," he said.

"I have to come clean to the police and talk about what Trill did. Whatever he has in mind, he has to be stopped."

"I agree," he said, and they rode in silence for a while.

By evening, they'd made it back to where the shooting had taken place. The wagon was gone as were humans and animals. The road was a mass of tracks from feet and wheels.

There was an unspoken agreement between them that they would keep going until they lost the light. They made it to the top of the cliff where Tyler told Julie about Meg Peterson's fall and her theory that it had been caused by whoever was after Julie.

"Did you check the horse and see if someone had somehow rigged her saddle or something to spook the horse?" she asked Tyler as they started down the switchbacks.

"I didn't have a chance. I hope someone else thinks to look. But really, I have a feeling Meg caused the accident when she waved at me and startled poor Snowflake. I have a sneaking suspicion she knew she'd done it because she's not as good a horsewoman as she pretended to be and she was embarrassed. I mean all that jolly Midwestern charm went up in smoke when she got hurt. She turned whiny and clingy."

"Is it a bad break?"

"I don't know. They should be back at the ranch by now so she'll be getting it fixed. Andy is the one I'm really worried about."

Julie nodded, silently agreeing. How many people had now been hurt because of her? James Killigrew, the real Dr. Robert Marquis, Nora, Andy, maybe Meg Peterson. Had they suffered because Julie was a coward afraid to face her mistakes? Was she what Tyler claimed she was—a quitter?

"You're awfully quiet," Tyler commented as they neared the bottom of the hill and entered Dead Man's Ravine.

"Just thinking," she said.

They stopped by the shack which Tyler opened by breaking the lock because the key was on the wagon. They gathered a few supplies and then continued on down to the creek at the bottom of the ravine where the welcoming sound of gurgling water perked the horses right up.

They unsaddled the horses who waded into the water and drank while Tyler started a fire. Julie filled one of the small dented pots they'd taken from the shack with water from the river and propped it on a rock to heat. If she could boil it long enough, it should be safe to drink. She looked through the canned food they'd gathered up at the shack—the selection wasn't great, but she was so hungry that even canned tamales and fruit cocktail sounded delicious.

For the first hour of darkness, they made the camp habitable, spreading out the bedroll, heating the tamales and eating them right out of the pan. They had found only one spoon, so they took turns fishing the fruit directly out of the can, and between the trilling water and fitful spitting of the fire, the flickering firelight and the carpet of stars overhead, Julie began to believe she was safe.

The light from the fire barely illuminated the creek, but after dinner, they took the sliver of soap and the one towel they'd found in the shack and walked down to the creek. Julie waded out breast-high wearing all her

clothes. They were filthy but she'd rather be wet than
take time to remove them. It was very dark so far out
in the water, cold and kind of eerie, the beach illuminated like a small stage. She dipped her head under the
water and tried to work up a lather with the soap. She
was rinsing her hair when she glanced toward shore
and saw Tyler standing on the beach, strong and naked.
Her stomach flipped. At least she thought it was her
stomach; the sensation might actually originate from
farther down.

Man, he was hot, his body perfect, the fitful light
thrown from the fire bathing all his muscles, a god of
sorts, a man in his element.

By the time she got out of the water, he'd towel-dried
and pulled on his jeans, and held his wet underwear in
one hand, his shirt in the other.

"You going to wear that shirt tonight?" she asked.

"No, you want it?"

"Please."

He handed it to her, staring down at her as he did so,
his eyes almost impossible to see because the firelight
was to his back. His gaze stirred a few embers inside
of her and her breath caught.

He handed her the towel next and told her he was
going to go stoke the campfire. She quickly stripped off
her clothes and put on his shirt, buttoning it with shaking fingers. Towel wrapped around her head, she wrung
the water out of her heavy, wet clothes, then gathered
them together and walked back up the gentle slope.

Tyler was in the process of draping his underwear
over the makeshift clothesline he'd created by string-
ing the lasso from Shasta's saddle between two trees.
"Allow me," he said, holding out a hand and she handed
him her wet garments. As she unwound the towel from

her hair, she watched him dangle her bra and panties over the rope with his two big hands. The same sensation his nudity had caused happened again, and this time there was no doubt about where it originated and what it meant.

"I shook out the bedroll," he said. "Can you stand the thought of getting back in it?"

She was trembling, but it wasn't the bedroll's fault. "Sure, we just won't zip it."

"You don't have to share it with me," he said. "I can sleep on the ground and use my saddle as a pillow."

She stared at him for a long, slow minute while summoning the courage to speak the truth. "I can't stop thinking about you," she said. "About us."

"Now just be careful," he said, "about what you say and how you say it. You know how I feel about you."

"Still, Tyler? After everything I've put you through?"

"Yes," he said.

His response was immediate and said with the simple sincerity she had always found so compelling. She smiled in spite of all the terrible things that had happened in the past week. "That first night in the barn—"

"Too fast," he said, shaking his head.

"Yes…and no," she said. "I told you it wasn't what I wanted, but I was lying."

"You were lying," he repeated. "Why?"

"Because I didn't know what making love would mean and I didn't want to hurt you again."

"It's too late to worry about that," he said.

"Are you sure?"

"Yes."

"Well, if you're going to sleep on the ground, you're going to need your shirt," she whispered, and began unbuttoning it, aware his gaze was glued to every movement she made until she shrugged the shirt off her shoulders. Standing there naked, she offered it to him.

He made a deep, sexy sound in his throat. "I have a better idea," he said, reaching for her.

Chapter Fourteen

Just touching her, holding her against him was almost more than he could bear. He wanted everything to be perfect for her, but it started out so fast and just seemed to go faster and faster like a runaway train. One minute he was clutching her backside to him, the next she had wrapped her legs around him and he was holding her and always, always their mouths were together, tongues exploring, the world reduced to warm, wet and wild.

He laid her down atop the bag and stripped off his jeans, then he straddled her, touching every inch of her fire-lit skin with his hands or his mouth or both. And she was all over him, freer with her body than she'd been for years, like the old Julie he'd married…and lost.

Thoughts like those, when they surfaced, were pushed away like a dangerous log jamming a fragile pier. There would be time to consider what all this meant later; for now he was content to be in the moment, making love to the woman he loved.

When at last they came together it was like an explosion took place within the confines of the bedroll and they lay sweaty and spent in each others arms, limbs entwined, out of breath and exhausted. He kissed her forehead a dozen times as her body gradually relaxed and her breathing became regular, planning on staying awake all night to keep watch or maybe just to extend the unity they'd rediscovered before the cold light of day split it asunder.

But the previous few nights caught up with him after a while and he felt his eyelids growing heavier and heavier as the fire quietly died down and the world shrank to just the two of them.

JULIE AWOKE WITH THE dawn and found herself still in Tyler's warm arms. For a while she watched him sleep, unsure if the night before had been the best of her life or the biggest mistake she'd ever made, or maybe a little of both.

As though sensing her gaze, his eyelids fluttered open. When their eyes met, he smiled and kissed her lips briefly. "Morning," he said.

"Morning."

"Have you been awake long?"

"No, just for a few minutes. But I think we should get up and start back to the ranch. I'm anxious about Andy and I know Rose must be worried sick about you."

He closed his arms around her. "Maybe there's time—"

"Get up, you lazy bum," she said.

He got out of the bedroll and stretched, treating her to his nude backside which she studied, enjoying the way his muscles flexed when he walked. He pulled his shorts off the line and slipped into them, then gathered her clothes and brought them to her. "I'll get some water to heat so we can at least wash our faces," he said, and grabbing the beat-up pot, sauntered down to the river.

Julie dressed quickly, her clothes mostly dry but cold from the cool morning temperature. Not that she was complaining. Hard not to compare this morning with the one from the day before when she'd woken up after a night trussed like a turkey, cold and stiff and lying on the dirt, without a glimmer of reasonable hope. She had been certain she was looking at her last day on earth yesterday, and yet here she was.

Thanks to Tyler...

As he finished dressing, she gathered wood for a small fire, then surveyed the last of the two cans they'd swiped from the shed. "Ravioli or chili for breakfast?" she called.

"Chili," he said. While she opened the can and dumped the contents in the pan, he tended the reluctant fire. They ate with a kind of shyness brought on by the memories of the passion they'd shared the night before. She was afraid he was going to want to talk about it, investigate her feelings, discuss what had changed and what hadn't and how they each felt about it, and she was too confused for such a talk. But as though he sensed her reluctance for that topic, he ate his chili without conversation.

After they'd eaten, they washed up, buried their refuse and gathered the horses for the ride home.

It took several hours of intense riding to get back to the river into which Julie had fallen, then a few more to get back to the site of their first camp. Tyler broke the lock on that shed, too, taking it out with a single shot. This time they found mostly canned fruit and ate it standing up, out of the can. A sealed plastic jug of water served to quench thirst and after a hurried meal, they were back in the saddle and headed out for the last leg of the trip.

"Do you think about the future much?" Julie asked Tyler as they neared the ranch.

"I used to," he said, darting her a quick glance. "It's

no secret I've wanted kids for a while now. The ranch needs a new infusion of Hunt blood."

"That means a lot to you, doesn't it?" she asked, and for the first time in a couple of days remembered the bomb John Smyth was getting ready to launch at Tyler.

"Sure. But not just to carry on the name. My own father died when I was a teenager. I missed a lot of good years with him, years I'd like to share with my own kids. How about you, Julie?"

"I want children, too," she said, surprised at the ease with which the words slipped out. But she'd thought her life was over, she'd seen no possibility of a future and now that there was one, she felt changed, different, as though there were avenues she wanted to explore, parts of herself that she'd been afraid to know.

He seemed equally surprised. "Really?" There was no ignoring the excited tone of his voice.

"Really." She needed to explain herself. "I tried to stop thinking about it when I left here," she added. "I wanted to immerse myself in the present. I'd tried so hard to fit into your life, Tyler, to want what you wanted, and it made me feel like the ultimate failure when I couldn't."

"There goes the little bubble I created in my head," he said, his lowered voice hard to hear over the sound of the horses' hooves.

"What do you mean?"

"I told myself to be cautious with you but of course, I didn't really listen."

"Oh, Tyler."

"No, it's okay," he said, holding up a hand. "You never promised me anything. The important thing is the danger is almost over for you. You'll have to stand up to Trill, but you won't have to do it alone. We can drive into the sheriff's office and find out what to do next. I guess we both need to learn to take life one day at a time."

One day at a time. What an easy concept and what a difficult path to follow...

She looked up at the century house as they drew parallel to it, her gaze zeroing in on the second-floor window of the room they'd shared up until a year ago. At first she thought it was the nature of their conversation that drew her attention in that direction and then she realized something was wrong.

For one thing, the curtains were fluttering in the wind which meant the window was open. Tyler never left the house open for days at a time when he wasn't on the ranch, not with strangers coming and going all the time. Then she realized there was something shiny behind the curtains....

"Tyler," she said quickly, "dig in your heels and ride like hell!"

Before either one of them could make this happen a shot fired out, then another and another. Julie felt a burning sensation in her arm and jumped from the horse. She was riding Tex, the roan, and the poor guy took off in a cloud of dust.

Tyler was soon at her side. He shooed the other two horses away, maybe using them as a diversion. He half carried her to the shelter of the fence where Julie knew they'd be invisible from the upstairs window. A hail of bullets danced around them.

"You've been hit," he said when they'd reached their destination.

"So have you," she said, touching his left forearm.

"It's just a scratch." He pulled his bandanna from

around his neck and pressed it against her wound. "Did you see someone?"

"Just the glint of something metallic."

He took out his gun.

"Go get 'em," she said, taking the bandanna and applying her own pressure. "I'll be fine. That has to be Trill in there and I don't want him to get away."

"Are you sure—"

"Hurry, Tyler, before he leaves. But be careful, he's a cop."

"Yeah, well, *I'm* a cowboy," he said. Then he was gone.

HE FIGURED HE HAD to have the advantage; after all, he had known this house his entire life and lived in it the past seven years. He found the back door open and hoped it meant the intruder had been careless getting into the house and not that he'd already left.

He knew where to stand in the foyer so that he could hear the creaking of the old floorboards if anyone upstairs moved. All but holding his breath, he stood there now, gun at the ready. After several tense seconds, he heard the squeak he'd been waiting for.

"Gotcha!" he whispered.

He started up the stairs avoiding the noisy third step and the last one, then crept along the hallway.

The gun went off again and he flattened himself against the wall, expecting a bullet in the head any second until he realized the fire had been directed outside, not inside. Julie! She must be doing something to attract the shooter's attention. He took the last few steps quickly, not worrying about noise as the gunman was still shooting up a storm.

The gunfire stopped as Tyler reached the bedroom

door. He could see a shape behind the curtain and from the furtive movement and sounds, guessed the gunman was reloading. Charging across the room, he threw himself at the shape and tackled it to the floor. The curtains came crashing down with them. A gun went off but the bullet flew by Tyler's head. Tyler grabbed the weapon and clicked on the safety, then stuffed it in his waistband. He got to his feet, pointing his own gun down at the gunman and took a deep breath.

"Get up," he said.

Julie came crashing into the room behind him. "Are you okay?"

"Stay back," he warned her. Who knew if the assailant carried another weapon? Right now, that person seemed to be having a lot of trouble fighting his way out of the folds of fabric. Tyler leaned down and grabbed an arm and pulled the gunman to his feet.

Tyler's mouth dropped open as the curtains slid away, revealing the cold gray eyes of the woman he knew as Meg Peterson. The kindly Midwestern glow was gone, replaced by a hard, menacing glare directed behind Tyler toward the door.

"You!" Julie said incredulously.

Meg laughed without mirth. "Who else, you fools?"

"OKAY, YES, ALL RIGHT, I made Snowflake go over the edge," Meg said. "I was the official diversion although I didn't plan on the stupid horse falling. Ted was positive he could handle the old man and the girl. Where is he?"

She was sitting on their bed. Tyler had called the sheriff's department who had promised to dispatch someone right away. He'd tied her up, hands behind her back. There was no sign of the supposed broken wrist. For good measure, he held a gun on her. She might look all-American wholesome, but that was about as real as the accent which had faded clean away.

"He's dead," Tyler said.

"You killed him?"

"Nope, snakes got him. Appropriate, isn't it? A snake in the grass getting bitten by a snake? A pit viper for a pit viper?"

"If you say so."

"Who was he? And who are you?"

"Ted is the only name I know for him, and Meg will do for me."

"Who hired you two?"

"I don't have to talk to you," she said.

"Did you have a contact on this ranch?"

"No, I don't think so—"

"He knew to target Robert Marquis. How?"

"I don't know," she insisted, "and even if I did, I wouldn't tell you."

"As far as I know, you haven't actually killed anyone yet. The fake doctor killed the real doctor and kidnapped—"

"Don't try that," she said with a look of disdain on her face. "I'm an accessory to everything and you probably know it. Okay, I'll tell you. What's the difference to me? The answer is, I don't know. I just know it's a man and he's traveling very soon to somewhere, and before you ask, no, I'm not privy to where. He's going to assassinate a political figure, and no, I don't know who that is either. Now, aren't you glad we had this little conversation?"

Julie came into the room. "I can't reach the professor," she said. Tyler knew she'd been downstairs using the phone to make a slew of calls, including one to Professor Killigrew to warn him about Trill.

"I called the ranch and explained the shots and the horses that showed up a little while ago. I told everyone to stay there and not to be surprised if they heard sirens."

"And did you tell them about her?" Tyler asked, nodding toward Meg.

"I just said she was with us. They hadn't missed her yet. Everyone thought she was in her room sleeping. Turns out her wrist is sprained, not broken."

"And what about Andy?" Tyler added, almost hating to hear the answer.

"He's still alive. They airlifted him to an urgent care facility. Mele went with him."

"Good. And Trill? Were you able to make sure he's still in Portland?"

"No. I called the station and asked to be put through to him although my plan was to hang up before he picked up his phone, but I was told he was unavailable for the next week and I should try his cell phone. What about her?" Julie added, looking hard at Meg. "Did she mention Trill's name?"

"How about it?" Tyler asked Meg. "Do you know a cop by the name of Roger Trill?"

"I make it a policy not to make friends with cops. I've never heard of Roger Trill."

"We think he's who hired you."

"Because I doubt I'm going to get paid for a job I didn't complete, it doesn't really matter to me."

"You might be able to save a man's life if you would just cooperate," Julie coaxed.

Meg shrugged. "All I know is the man who hired me is a terrorist, an assassin with connections. Ted met him last year at some convention or something."

Julie and Tyler exchanged a look, then moved back

toward the wall. Keeping the gun pointed at Meg, they exchanged a hurried, whispered conversation. "The convention part fits with Trill," Julie said.

"And with your old boss. Wait, why couldn't you get a hold of Killigrew? Doesn't he carry a phone with him?"

"Yes, but he doesn't always answer it, especially when he doesn't recognize the caller and he would have no way of associating me with this number. For that matter, if he did, that might be enough to keep him from answering it."

"How about his office? Can someone there get in touch with him?"

"Not if he hasn't replaced me yet. I know he's gone because I got the usual message he hooks up when he leaves. He's a private man, Tyler. He takes off on these trips to broaden his horizons, as he calls it. He stays in a room by himself when he isn't networking."

"I wonder if the reason he reacted so strongly to your snooping is because Trill is blackmailing him. Maybe he thought you were in on it."

She nodded. "That makes sense."

Julie moved closer to Meg. "Do you know why someone wants to kill me?"

Again Meg shrugged. "What's it to me?"

They both looked up when they heard a siren approaching. "I'll go let the sheriff in," Julie said, and left the room.

Tyler stared at Meg who met his look with a defiant one of her own.

"You and Ted were partners?"

"Not really. We'd worked together before. He called me and told me to get out here a day before him and pose as something harmless. I was his backup plan if he wasn't successful making Julie's death appear an accident."

"Why was it so important it appear an accident?" he asked.

"Because that's what the client asked for. You know how it goes. You get a contract and you try to fulfill the terms, but the bottom line was actually really simple. Kill Julie. One way or another."

"And you failed," Tyler said.

She stared at him. "Nobody's perfect," she said with a bitter smile.

Chapter Fifteen

"Let me get this straight," the officer said. His eyes were all but spinning as he held out his pointer finger, counting things down. "There's a doctor's body stuffed in the trunk of a car in the long-term parking lot in Chicago?"

When Julie nodded and opened her mouth to speak, he held up a pudgy hand. Deputy Harris was a nice man, but Julie got the feeling his office wasn't used to handling anything like what they were getting now. "Please, ma'am," he said, "don't talk, let me finish." He added his middle finger. "There's another dead guy named Ted something up on Willard land who died by stepping in a nest of rattlesnakes. In June, no less."

Julie nodded again.

His ring finger joined the other two. "Then there's a dead woman in Portland, a victim of a robbery, only you say she was really killed by a police detective working undercover who was also blackmailing your old boss?"

"I think so," she said.

He shook his head and popped out his little finger. "Plus the woman we just took into custody and the dead guy with the snakes are killers hired by this same detective to kill you because you figured out he was really a cop and not a federal agent of some kind and now your old boss is in danger because the detective is on vacation, so I should call Seattle and have this Killigrew man alerted?"

"And arrest Trill. I'm sure he's there, too."

The deputy stared at her hard, opened his whole hand and shook it. "Ma'am, I have heard me some stories, I surely have, but this one beats 'em all. Tell you what. You and the other folks who were on that cattle drive stay right here on this ranch. We'll go recover the snake-bite victim and come back here tomorrow and go over this all again."

"But, Deputy, there isn't time—"

"We'll do this my way. Now, I'll make some calls. Just hold tight until tomorrow."

Without waiting for a response, he pulled on his hat and addressed the others. "Stay put for a couple more days, folks, then I'm sure you can go home."

"Most of us have travel plans for the weekend," John Smyth said amid a chorus of assents.

"That works out fine, then." The deputy nodded at Julie and Tyler and walked out of the room. Julie stared at his back, but she didn't say anything. She thought Tyler might, but he seemed anxious to leave and hustled out of the room.

Rose took over. "We have additional guests here, so it'll be a full house tonight, just like the old days. Surf and turf for dinner, folks, in one hour. Now, where'd Heidi get off to?"

"She wanted to talk to Tyler about something," Mele said.

Julie could tell John was about to come speak to her and she didn't want to encourage that, so she left quietly, following Rose as though planning to help. She hated keeping secrets from Tyler and the knowledge of what John planned on dropping on Tyler weighed heavily on her heart. For that reason she grabbed a snack and skipped out the kitchen door, making it back to cabin eight where she planned on taking a rejuvenating hot shower before she did something she knew would hurt Tyler to the quick.

She had to leave. Tonight. Soon. She could not sit here in Montana while Professor Killigrew walked into a trap in Seattle. The deputy would not act until it was too late. She'd made Killigrew's original arrangements, she knew where the professor was staying and that he would meet with a committee tomorrow night at the hotel. She also knew leaving like this would infuriate and hurt Tyler and hoped he understood that at least this time she wasn't running away from trouble, but straight into it.

When she turned off the water after brushing her teeth, she heard the faint sound of a familiar tune and exited the bathroom to find Tyler sitting on the bed with his boots off.

He stopped humming. "I've always loved the way you look wrapped up in a towel," he said. He'd obviously bathed, too, and had changed into casual clothes. He looked familiar and sexy and wonderful.

"You didn't stay for your dinner?" she asked.

"Not hungry—well, not for food," he said, making the most of the double entendre by pitching his voice just so and lavishing her with his gaze. "Anyway, Mom is as tense as a calf at branding time. John Smyth is acting funny and everyone wants to hear about the snakes over and over again. I swear, you'd think they're all disappointed they missed the last part of the 'adventure.'"

She smiled and sat down next to him.

"I talked to Heidi," he said suddenly, leaning forward, his attention apparently galvanized on her shoulders. She felt a hot, piercing stab of desire.

"What about?" she asked, her voice raspy, her skin electrified.

"When she heard about the real Dr. Marquis being murdered, she asked me if we could speak. She remembered a call from a couple of days before the trip. That would have made it right around the time everything happened to you in Portland. Someone convinced her to give him the names of the people coming to the ranch. He claimed he was writing a story and the ranch would get lots of free publicity and he wanted contacts. She blithely asked if the guest list for the cattle drive in two days would be good and he said that would be fine. So, she gave it to him and forgot all about it."

As he'd been talking, he'd been studying her. With his last words, he leaned forward a little bit more, lifted her hair away from her shoulders and kissed her neck, effectively melting her internal organs.

"Then there was no one here in league with those two murderers," she mumbled.

"Just a kid who didn't think," he said as his fingers skimmed across her shoulders, up her throat, then down under the towel which fell away from her body. She closed her eyes as he found a dozen ways to touch her that glued her to the bed.

Soon they were under the cool sheets making their own heat. Julie knew this was just going to make everything even more difficult, but she honestly didn't care. She needed him and he needed her and tomorrow she'd never see him again.

Afterward, she realized she had to find a way to get him out of her cabin because she had to leave. She'd swiped the truck keys from the century house, but how to get out of this room....

Turning in his arms, she looked up at his face and found him staring at her as his hand caressed her arm.

"When were you going to tell me?" he asked.

She studied his eyes and didn't speak. Was he talking about the adoption thing?

"Were you just going to sneak away?" he added.

She pulled back a little when she realized this had nothing to do with John Smyth. He obviously guessed her plans. "Yes. How did you know?" she asked.

"Two things. First, the expression on your face when the deputy told you to stay put, and second, my extra truck keys are sitting over there on the bureau."

She looked at the chest. Sure enough, there were the keys where she'd dumped them out of her pocket before her shower. "Well, good. I'm glad you know. Now I can be up-front and ask properly. May I borrow your truck?"

"No."

She narrowed her eyes. "I have to go to Seattle, Tyler. I have to find the professor. If anything happens to him—"

He interrupted her by putting a finger across her lips. "You may not borrow my truck, but I will take you there myself."

"What? You can't leave now with things like they are around here—"

"Like hell I can't."

"But Tyler—"

"No buts, Julie. That's the deal. Me and the truck or you walk. Sorry, babe, sometimes a man just has to draw a line in the sand."

"Why, you—"

This time he shut her up with a kiss.

TYLER INSISTED THEY tell someone where they were going and Julie convinced him to let her tell Rose while he went back to the century house and packed a bag. She found Rose in the kitchen supervising the dishes. Rose led her back to her suite and closed the door behind them.

"I don't have much time," Julie said quickly. "Tyler and I are leaving right now."

"You're going to Seattle, aren't you?"

"I have to."

"And he's going with you?"

"Yes. I tried to talk him out of it, but—"

"But he loves you."

"I know."

Rose grabbed her hand as tears sprang into her eyes. "Julie, John Smyth told you his preposterous idea, didn't he?"

Julie returned the pressure on Rose's trembling hand. "Did he finally talk frankly with you?"

"Yes, earlier today. I told him to leave at once, but then you and Tyler showed up and now he can't leave even if he wants to." She closed her eyes and took a steadying breath. "I knew he was up to no good. That's why I didn't go on the cattle drive, but now look at all that's happened."

"None of that is your fault," Julie said. "Just tell me this. Is what he thinks even possible?"

Slowly, Rose nodded.

"Please try not to worry," Julie said. "I trust John to do what's best for Tyler and I trust Tyler to always know who loves him. You won't lose him if what John says is true. You'll explain the past to him and he'll understand."

"Can you promise me that?" Rose asked.

Julie looked her straight in the eyes. "Yes, I can promise you that."

JULIE DROVE FIRST WHILE Tyler did his best to shut down his brain and get some sleep. His turn behind the wheel would come soon enough. He didn't awaken until Julie stopped the truck at a gas station. As the attendant filled the tank, she stifled a yawn.

"My turn," he said, getting out of the truck and walking around to the driver's door. He opened it for her and caught her in his arms as she got out, hugging her against him, smiling inside when she hugged him back. He'd been dreaming about her minutes before, and touching her now made him burn for her.

After fourteen hours of driving, they arrived in Seattle at noon or a little after. It took another hour to navigate the city traffic to get to the hotel where Julie had booked Killigrew a room. Her plan was simple. Stake out his room until she saw him, convince him his life was in danger and he needed to seek police protection, leave.

"They're not going to tell us which room he's staying in, you know," Tyler pointed out as they entered the parking garage. "Even if you tell them it's an emergency, the most they'll do is send up a message. Maybe."

"I know. That's why you're going to put in a rushed order for flowers to be delivered asap. I'll follow the delivery person up to the professor's room."

"I can't order flowers for another man," he said, looking a little horrified.

"Sure you can. Hurry up now, if I remember the information on the internet site, the florist is right off the lobby." The elevator opened and she pointed to the far left. "Over there. Make it something different so we can be sure to know which one goes to his room. I'm going to look in the café and make sure he's not eating lunch or something."

Tyler walked into the florist shop alone and picked up the first arrangement that caught his eye, a towering bamboo and orchid thing. He invented a story about an ailing friend and gave a fifty-dollar tip for immediate delivery.

Leaving the shop, he spotted Julie seated over by what appeared to be the freight elevator. She'd asked him to let her go alone and even though he didn't like the idea, what choice did he have? It was difficult to remember she was not his to shelter and protect when every bone in his body ached to do just that.

So he sat close by on a lounge chair in the quaint kind of old-fashioned lobby where a sign three feet in front of him said "Emerald City Discussion Attendees. Meet and Greet downstairs in Coho Room starting at 5:00 p.m. Committees forming tomorrow evening at nine."

Julie had asked him to keep his eyes peeled for a taller-than-average man of fifty or so years with wild white hair. If he came back, John was to follow him in case the flower trick didn't work.

Fifteen minutes later, a young guy in a hotel uniform went into the flower shop and emerged carrying the orchid arrangement. He went right to the freight elevator, just as though he'd rehearsed his role, and got inside. The elevator was the kind with a panel of numbers on the outside that lit as the elevator traveled. Tyler saw it pause on the eighth floor. Julie apparently did as well. She dashed around to the guest elevator and disappeared inside.

To hell with her damn plan, he decided as he got to his feet and crossed the lobby. To hell with respecting her wishes.

JULIE GOT OFF THE elevator and wasted valuable time attempting to orientate herself. Where was the blasted freight elevator in this maze of halls? She was pretty sure she'd blown it when she sighted the bellboy walking past the end of the hallway she currently occupied. He still held the orchids.

When he was out of sight, she ran down the hall and arrived at the crossroads in time to see him stop in front of a door. He knocked smartly twice, waited a second and then the door opened. Julie heard the rumble of male voices, the flowers disappeared, money exchanged hands and the bellboy walked by again, his eyes glued to the screen of his phone where he busily texted a message.

But now she knew which room. She walked up to the door and raised her hand, pausing when motion down the hall caught her attention. Turning, she saw Tyler walking toward her. A brief flash of irritation came and went. She knew Killigrew was in his room—that's all that mattered now.

She opened her mouth and he put a finger over his own lips. She walked to join him instead.

"Did you find him?"

"Yes. He's in his room. I was just about to knock."

"He'll see you through the peephole."

"I know, but he'll be curious—"

"Just let me stand in front of the door—you stand off to the side." He took out his gun and handed it to her. "We're breaking some pretty serious laws by carrying a concealed weapon, but we don't know for sure he's alone, do we?"

She hadn't thought about that.

"You hold on to the gun and stand to the side of the door. Let's go."

There he was, giving orders. Funny thing was, however, she didn't mind. He'd made some good points, so they set themselves up as he'd suggested. Tyler knocked. The door opened wide.

Holding the gun out of sight, Julie was ready to step into view, but Tyler raised his hands by his head. "You aren't the professor," he said.

Julie shrank back against the wall.

"And you're not anyone I know," the other voice said. Julie knew that voice. Roger Trill! Her fingers tightened around the grip.

"Do you always hold a gun on strangers?" Tyler asked.

"Just when they're friends of Killigrews," he said. "Get in here."

There was no time to think. Once that door closed, Tyler would be at the mercy of Roger Trill, and when he found out who Tyler was, his life wouldn't be worth a plugged nickel. Julie stepped closer. Apparently sensing her thoughts, Tyler grabbed his side and bent over double, groaning as though he was in sudden, intense pain. Trill's hand reached out and grabbed Tyler's arm as if to pull him inside, and part of his head showed as he did so. Quickly flipping on the safety and turning the gun in her hand, Julie brought the grip down on Trill's temple. He yelled. Tyler tackled him. Julie ran into the room and pointed the gun as Tyler disarmed the other man. Trill was subdued without a shot being fired.

He sat on the floor, rubbing the knot on his temple. His eyes narrowed when he saw Julie. "I didn't expect to see *you*," he said.

Julie stared him right in the eyes. "Because you thought your hired killers would get to me first? Well, they failed."

His pinched face registered confusion. "What hired killers?"

"The two you sent to Montana to kill me."

He shook his head. "Not me. Probably your boss. He sent killers? That's rich, isn't it? Guess his mind was on more important things to bother with you himself."

"Sure. First you pushed me under a bus—"

"Okay, that *was* me. I panicked when I learned via the wiretap that you knew I was a phony agent. When I saw you at the police station, I thought you knew it was me."

"And you killed Nora—"

"No."

"I was on the phone when you came to ask her to check my apartment. I've spoken to her brother. I know."

Flinching, he quickly looked away. "I didn't kill her," he said.

"Yes, you did," she said. "Don't lie."

He shook his head, met her gaze, looked away. "I could tell she knew I'd taken the suitcase," he said. "I came back just to scare her, and she tried to call the police and I hit her. It was an accident, that's all. I didn't mean to kill her."

He rubbed his eyes and when he once again met their gaze, his face appeared paler and more pinched than ever. "I'm in over my head, I admit that. The gambling has taken over, I'm making some terrible choices and I thought if I could just get proof Killigrew is the assassin I know he is, I could make some money, pay off some debts before my life is ruined."

Julie shook her head. "Killigrew is the assassin? Not you?"

"Hell, no, not me. I've suspected him for a long time. I've tried to catch him. Last year I arranged to run into him at a conference, even got our picture taken together."

"Why? And how did he end up with a copy?"

"I sent it to him. I just wanted him to get nervous. Listen, whether he takes me out or the loan shark does, what does it matter? I was just trying to find a way under his skin. But the man is an ice cube."

"There were four men in that photograph," Julie said. "One was Ted, a hired killer who it appears worked with Killigrew in some capacity. Who was the other?"

"Ignacio Lendez. President Lendez's son, you know, the old president of Uruguay who left office last year after his kid's 'untimely' death. Ignacio was killed by a little pellet filled with poison that has no antidote, kind of like back in the seventies when the Bulgarians filled a tiny metal sphere with a biotoxin called ricin and stabbed it into Georgi Markov's leg. Ignacio died a couple of days later. Your boss did it."

"That's impossible!" Julie said.

"I knew he was getting ready for another job," Trill continued. "There's a meeting going on in Seattle that has nothing to do with this conference. Something where a dozen leaders of South American countries are getting together for some powwow on democracy. I was trying to pump you to find out who his target is—"

"So you can blackmail Killigrew?" Tyler snapped as he took the gun from Julie. "I should shoot you now and save the government the cost of your trial."

"It's the addiction, man," Trill said.

"You knew about a murderer and your plan was to make money off him instead of bring him to justice? That's not addiction, that's a corrupt soul." Tyler shook his head and added, "Julie, look around this room. Your boss isn't staying here."

Now that she was no longer holding the gun, Julie did just that and realized Tyler was right. Besides the orchids, which had been deposited on a low table, there was no sign of occupancy.

"He never stays in the room he books," Trill said and produced a dry laugh. "He checks in, changes his appearance and leaves the hotel as a whole different person."

"Then why are you here?"

"I was hoping he'd left a clue as to the identity of his next target. He specializes in South American policy makers who rub his client's interests the wrong way. One of those twelve men gathering tonight isn't going to live to see next week."

"But why tonight?"

"Because tomorrow the sessions start and it'll be almost impossible to get near any of the attendees. No, he'll do it tonight. I should have just gone there and taken a million pictures and pieced it together later. I shouldn't have come to his room."

"You're right," Julie said. "You shouldn't have."

He produced another little laugh. "When the job is done, Killigrew will disappear back into his scholarly role as educator of the young. Face it, Ms. Chilton, when he finds out his hired killers blew it, you don't stand much of a chance seeing next week either."

Chapter Sixteen

Tyler wanted to call the police, but Julie convinced him it would take them too long to respond. Just convincing them they weren't nuts, especially in lieu of Trill's status as a cop, would destroy any chances they had to stop Killigrew. After Tyler gagged Trill and bound him to a chair using the drapery cords and Trill's own handcuffs, Julie took Trill's phone. They put the do-not-disturb sign on Killigrew's door as they left.

"If we survive this day, there's going to be a lot of questions to answer," Tyler said. "Like kidnapping a policeman, carrying a concealed weapon, swiping a cell phone. What do you want the phone for anyway?"

"I can access the internet with this phone and find out where the meeting is taking place. And I can call Killigrew's old assistant. She might be able to tell me something that would help us figure out how Killigrew disguises himself. He's not an ordinary-looking man, Tyler. He's tall and distinguished-looking, kind of haughty in his way. People don't look past him. How could he really be what Trill says he is?"

"Trill seemed pretty sure of himself."

"Still."

She tapped keys and scanned the internet until she finally said, "Eureka! The meeting starts tomorrow at the Pacific Sound Institute down near the wharf. Tonight there's a ticket-only cocktail party held at the same venue. I'll see if I can buy tickets online."

She poked around a little more and sighed. "It's been sold out for weeks."

"Now what?"

"I guess we go watch the arrivals. Now to find Marti Keizer."

That turned out to be surprisingly easy with one of the people search engines. "Here it is. Martina and Frederick Keizer, 211 Bay Street, Seaside, Oregon." As Tyler pulled into a parking lot, Julie punched in the phone number and, miracle of miracles, the phone was soon answered by a man.

"I'm looking for Marti Keizer," she said. Nerves were beginning to assert themselves as she tried to figure out how to ask Marti about Killigrew without alarming her.

"This is her husband. Who is this?" the man asked.

"She doesn't know me, Mr. Keizer. I took her old job. I just had a question—"

"What kind of crank are you?" he asked.

"I'm sorry," she said, alarmed. "After she retired—"

"Marti spent two whole days retired before she was killed while getting money from the ATM. If you are who you say you are, why didn't Killigrew tell you that?"

"I don't know, sir. I'm so sorry."

"We bought a beach house over here when she got that big payoff. We still hadn't unpacked the boxes when she was killed. I just stayed here, never went back to the city. They never caught the person who took her life...." His voice choked up and he added, "She was only fifty-eight years old. Damn." And he hung up.

"What is it?" Tyler asked as she clicked off the phone.

She looked at him. "Marti is dead. Murdered a couple of days after she left her job. Killigrew never mentioned it."

"Didn't the other people in the office say anything?"

"There are hardly any other people around. The professor kept a really low profile at the school and only one other woman worked in the office. She's a generation older than me and would hardly give me the time of day. I gathered it was because she figured she should have gotten the job I took, so I avoided her."

By THE TIME JULIE and Tyler found a parking spot and walked quickly back to the Pacific Sound Institute, cars had begun to pull into the portico to let off their occupants.

Some of the vehicles came equipped with flags, which they assumed held the diplomats from different countries. Being as there were no movie stars, the media attention was modest with just one news truck, a cameraman and a reporter hovering near the entrance. Pedestrians dressed in street clothes had stopped to watch and Julie and Tyler joined them.

Once people disembarked, they tended to blur together, some stopping to talk to the reporter, others standing off to the side looking relatively uncomfortable with the attention.

"That's the Uruguay car," Tyler said, pointing out a long black car with twin blue-and-white-striped flags each sporting a sunburst in the corner. The flags were affixed to the front bumper on either side.

Julie stared at the flags, then down the row of cars waiting their turn to unload. One car had the horizontal stripes of red, yellow and green—Bolivia's flag, she thought—and two down from that sported flags of green almost bisected by red-and-yellow chevrons set one upon the other.

She put her hand on Tyler's sleeve. "Look."

"What am I looking at?"

"Those flags. They remind me of the doodles in Killigrew's notebook. What country is that one with the green field?"

"I'm not sure. Guyana, I think."

"That has to be it. Killigrew's victim is in that car."

"And so are the diplomat's bodyguards. If we approach from the street, they'll probably shoot first and ask for ID second."

"But when the man gets out of that car, Killigrew is going to have to be close by, right? All he has to do is poke the man with something, mumble an apology and get away." They angled their way through the gathered crowd, arriving close enough to witness the unloading process when the Bolivian car disgorged a tall, handsome man and a woman equally as attractive.

The Guyana car was two down in line.

As Tyler inched closer, trying to be on hand when the diplomat disembarked, Julie studied the people around her.

How would Killigrew disguise himself? He couldn't make himself shorter unless he stooped or maybe he wore lifts while being a professor. She'd never noticed his shoes looking odd, so she looked for a person kind of slumped over. His hair was his signature, so she could assume no white hair to suggest his own. *Look for darker hair or hats.* It was Seattle, in June—everyone was wearing a scarf or hat. Even the bag lady with the shopping cart looked bundled up.

A man standing behind the woman carried an um-

brella, also a pretty common sight in the Pacific Northwest. Wasn't that how the pellet that killed Georgi
Markov had been delivered, via a jab with the tip of
an umbrella? This guy had dark hair and a mustache,
glasses, a large nose…and was leaning heavily on the
umbrella. He wore a shapeless trench coat and a fedora.
He was about the right size.…

Julie moved that direction. That had to be Killigrew,
and she was gripped with the need to stop him. As she
got closer, he stepped forward. She twisted her head to
see where the Guyana car was and found the door had
been opened and an average-looking man of Latin descent wearing a black tuxedo had emerged. He paused
to adjust his cuffs. Julie looked back at the man she'd
targeted as Killigrew and found he'd paused and was
once again leaning on the umbrella. Behind him, the
bag lady flipped back a corner of the blanket that covered a shopping cart stuffed with odds and ends and
castoffs. Julie stared transfixed at the old woman's hand.

Julie made an intuitive leap. As the bag lady closed
her fingers around what appeared to be a harmless me-
chanical pencil, Julie backtracked. The bag lady was
moving again, this time quickly, the pencil all but hidden in her big hand, her movements seemingly random but taking her right into the path of the Guyana
diplomat.

"Tyler!" Julie yelled, and dozens of heads turned
her way, but not the woman's. "Watch out. It's the bag
lady. It's in a pencil." Tyler stepped in front of the diplomat, which alarmed the man's bodyguard and the police. Julie, unencumbered, ran to the diplomat. The bag
lady stopped just two feet away.

"She's going to kill you," Julie said, unsure if the

man even spoke English. "You mustn't let her touch you."

The police had started to pay attention to Julie, who yelled out another warning. Eyes turned to the bag lady and Julie cried, "That's not an old woman, it's an assassin. He's got poison—"

The bag lady looked right at Julie, but it was with Killigrew's eyes. He grabbed Julie and hissed in her ear. "You'll get it instead, you troublemaker."

And then Tyler was suddenly there. He struggled with Killigrew, who levered the pencil at Julie, choking her in the process as she pushed against the arm and the little point of the pencil that was getting closer with each beat of her heart. Tyler pulled his arm in the other direction, but the point kept coming. Then Julie heard a hiss issue from Killigrew's mouth as Tyler kicked him hard.

All of a sudden, Killigrew let go of Julie. She didn't know why, just that his arm slipped from her throat. She turned quickly to make sure Tyler was all right. He stood there staring at Killigrew, who had fallen to his knees and now gaped at his hand. The pencil stuck out of his palm, its deadly mission under way inside his own body.

THEY STAYED IN SEATTLE three days to answer a seemingly endless slew of questions. Killigrew refused to utter a word and died at the end of the second day without ever revealing anything. But Trill had amassed a lot of the information and was trying to buy his way into a plea bargain for causing Nora's death by spilling his guts.

The days were spent with the police, but the nights belonged to them. Tyler began to hope that a miracle was happening and that Julie was at last finding in their relationship what he'd always found—excitement, fulfillment, love. The admiration for her tenacity that had begun to grow out on the cattle drive just escalated as he watched her maneuver her way through a quagmire of legalese.

And then she got a phone call, and by the end of the call he could tell something had changed. Still, she didn't say anything and he was afraid to ask. Instead, he watched with interest as she dressed for dinner, wrapping herself in a new red dress that clung to every curve.

"That call today?" she said, as she buttered a roll at dinner. They'd both settled on Seafood Louies, crisp greens mounded with Dungeness crab and tender pink shrimp.

Tyler's stomach tensed at the tone in her voice. She was nervous and that made him nervous.

"It was from the chancellor at the school where Killigrew taught. Where I used to work."

"Did he want to congratulate you on your help for catching an assassin?" Tyler asked, fork poised over his dinner, appetite gone.

"Kind of. Actually, he offered me a job in his office."

"You're not going to take it, are you?"

She avoided looking at him when she responded. "Tyler, try to understand. If I go back to Montana now, I go as someone who failed miserably at making my way. This is my chance for redemption, my chance to prove to myself I can do it."

He pushed his plate away. "Listen to yourself," he said. "You've spent the past week outwitting murderers. You survived and you did it while working your tail off, by thinking on your feet, by facing every day."

"I'm alive because of you," she said.

"Don't sell yourself short."

She shook her head and he could see that he'd lost her—again.

The next day he drove her to Portland and kissed her while standing on the sidewalk out in front of her place. There was no way he was going inside her apartment. "As soon as I get home, I'll sign the papers," he assured her.

"Not now," she said. "Let me come visit you at the end of the season when we've both had time to think. We can talk then. You have a lot to do when you get back…."

"I don't need to think," he said. "I guess that's the difference between us."

"Tyler, try to understand. I have a chance for another new beginning here."

"You're fond of new beginnings, aren't you?" he muttered.

"Aren't you?"

"Not when I already have what I want," he said.

She squeezed his hand. "Call me when you get home. Let me know you arrived safely."

"Okay," he managed to say and then he had to leave or she'd hear his voice crack. He made a slight detour but otherwise drove straight through, unwilling to sleep, knowing what his dreams would be like if he did. As he switched off his key, he pulled out the replacement cell phone he'd bought in Seattle and dialed the number Julie had programmed into it.

"You made it," she said.

"Just got here."

"Everything okay?"

"Peachy," he said, and got out of the truck. "Listen, John Smyth and my mother are coming out of the house. Glory be, she's actually smiling at him. Anyway, they're on their way over so I'm hanging up. Take care of yourself, Julie." He broke the connection, preferring that to hearing her say goodbye…again.

"You still hanging around?" Tyler asked John.

"I'd planned to leave day before yesterday, but I read about what happened in Seattle and thought it would be worth it to hear the real story. Rose convinced me I wouldn't be any bother for a few more days and said you might need some help around here, what with Andy still in the hospital."

"Yeah. I stopped by and saw him on the way home. He's doing pretty good. Doctor says you and Mele saved his life."

"She did all the work," John said as Rose reached out and hugged Tyler. Her eyes asked the question he knew she wouldn't utter out loud and he hoped the modest shake of his head answered it. *Julie wasn't coming back*….

For the next few days, John helped out more and more at the ranch and Tyler began to suspect John was angling for a job. "What exactly is it you do when you're not playing cowboy?" he asked as John helped him load fence posts.

"This and that," John said.

"Don't you have a job?"

"Yeah, I have a job. Right now it's trying to put my family together again."

"Wife leave you?" Tyler asked, realizing suddenly that John never talked about himself.

"No, the one I want hasn't consented to marry me quite yet. She told me to take care of business and then make her my bride. I'm kind of anxious to get back to her, so I guess I better stop stalling and take care of business."

"Now you're talking in riddles," Tyler said. "Or circles. Why do I get the feeling you're trying to tell me something?"

"Because I'm trying to tell you something," John said. He dropped the four-by-four he'd hefted and sat down on the rear of the truck, lifting the water jug and taking a long swallow. Tyler pitched the post he'd lifted into the bed of the truck and sat down beside him. "What's up?"

John pushed back his hat. "I'm going to give you the abbreviated version first, let you assimilate that, then you can ask me anything you want and I'll answer you if I can. First I'll tell you a little about myself. My mother died when I was a kid. My father remarried and they had two children back to back, several years younger than me. Dad was a diplomat in a little country called Kanistan. Heard of it?"

"Sure," Tyler said, pouring cool water from his jug over the back of his neck. It felt great on his overheated skin.

"Well, as you know…" John began, but his words petered off. Tyler turned to see what had drawn his attention and found a small white car with Oregon plates coming down the gravel road. It pulled into the yard and stopped. The driver got out, the wind catching at her hair.

Tyler was suddenly on his feet. "We'll pick this up later, okay?" he said and walked toward the car, only vaguely aware of John's presence behind him. What was Julie doing here? He stopped short of her car and they stared at each other.

John walked by on his way back to the house. "Hello, Julie," he called as he passed.

Her answering hello sounded as distracted as Tyler felt.

She kept coming until she was standing close enough to touch. Brushing her hair from her amazing eyes, she stared up at him. His breathing became labored. For the first time in years, her eyes didn't seem to harbor any secrets and he didn't know what that meant.

"I've been doing a lot of thinking," she said.

"You're good at that."

"Yes, I guess I am. But sometimes I overthink things."

It grew silent again, and Tyler waited. He could see her struggling to find words. What was with everyone today?

"You know," he said, "John and I were just talking. He's got something on his mind and he's trying to get it out, but he started his story way back when he was a kid. I'm sure he'll wrap it all up eventually, but there's something to be said for just coming out and saying whatever it is you want to say."

"You mean stop beating around the bush."

"That's exactly what I mean. Start with why you're here."

"Did you sign the papers yet?"

"The divorce papers? Not exactly. You came all the way here for that?"

"Not exactly."

"Julie—"

"I came because I love you, Tyler. I always have and I think I always will."

"That's not good enough," he said.

Her eyes flashed. "I beg your pardon?"

"I want more than just your love."

Her hands landed on her waist and he realized she looked different than she had the first time she came back. She wasn't a whole lot bigger, but somehow, there was *more* of her. "What *do* you want?" she said.

He narrowed his eyes. "Let's just put it this way. You're heavy maintenance, Julie Hunt. You're just way too much work for a simple cowboy like me."

"But I'm worth it," she said.

He cracked a smile.

"And you like a challenge."

His smile widened. "Well, that's true, I do."

"And I don't want to go on without you."

"What about your new beginning? What about proving yourself?"

Her nose scrunched up. "Funny thing about that. I walked into the chancellor's office and looked at my pretty desk and listened to his grand plans and I realized I wasn't listening to him at all, that my heart was not in his office, not in that school, not in that state. It was here. I thought about Babylon. And this ranch. And Rose and cattle drives and the century house and how we could redo it to make it more modern. But most of all I thought about you and how you stuck with me and how much I wanted someday soon to look into your eyes and tell you I was pregnant with our first child. I want my life back, Tyler, and it took until two days ago to realize that my life is you and this ranch and this sky and—"

His voice gravelly with emotion, he interrupted her. "Why are you still standing all the way over there?" he asked, and opened his arms as she flew into his embrace.

Epilogue

Rose broke out the champagne and shooed everyone out of the kitchen but Julie and Tyler and for some reason John Smyth, whom she seemed to have taken a shine to. Tyler sat where she told him to sit and he realized there was something more than joy and celebration in the air...there was also expectation.

"You got us all arranged. What's going on?" Tyler asked, looking first at Julie, then at John.

"John has something important to tell you," Rose said.

A little gasp escaped Julie's lips. *Uh-oh...*

John rubbed his chin. "I started talking to you about this earlier today," John said.

"Yeah, I know," Tyler said cautiously. "You were telling me about a country called Kanistan."

"That's right."

"And about your mother dying when you were young and your father remarrying and having two more kids."

"Yeah. Well, unfortunately, my father and stepmother died in an explosion. I was injured in the blast and wound up with amnesia. I was raised by people claiming to be my grandparents. Last year I was contacted by a woman who'd seen my picture when it showed up in the newspaper after I saved the life of a congressman.

She said I looked just like her dead brother. She'd been told his three sons died, but now she wondered if one of them was alive—in other words, me. Was it possible the other two were, as well?"

John took a deep breath as he glanced at each of them in turn. "You have to understand that was the first time in my life since I was ten that I realized I even had brothers. I went to Kanistan and did some research and met roadblocks and then came home, planning to return, but before I could, someone from there came here to shut me up. The result was that I got amnesia on top of the original amnesia."

"Are you making this up?" Tyler said. His mother and Julie were very quiet.

"No. I don't blame you for thinking that, though. Now, tell me this. Where did you pick up that tune you whistle?"

Tyler whistled a few bars. "That?"

"Yeah, that."

"I don't know. I've always whistled it." He looked at his mother for confirmation and she nodded. "I think I made it up," he added.

"You didn't," John said. "In fact it's a Kanistan song that was popular twenty-five or thirty years ago. Our father had a man working for him—"

"Wait just a second," Tyler said, jumping to his feet. "*Our* father?"

"Hear me out. This man worked at the embassy and he visited the house often. He always whistled that song. That's where you heard it. You're my younger brother."

"Because of a song? Man, you're crazy. There's no way we can be related. For one thing, I'm not adopted—"

"Yes, you are," Rose said softly. "I know I should

have told you years ago, but your father was adamant and then after he died, it just seemed like it was too late."

"You knew my parents were murdered?" Tyler said. Had the world just gone crazy? He looked at Julie and found her eyes flooded with sympathy.

"No, of course she didn't," John said. "The man responsible for this was very clever. He changed your name and falsified your records and shipped you away where you couldn't cause him any trouble. Rose and your adoptive dad got a whole different story about your background."

"We were told your father and mother died in a traffic accident that you survived and that's why you were so scared when you got here."

"It's the same story my fake grandparents told everyone in the town where I was raised," John said. "Standard issue, I guess."

Rose had gotten to her feet. Tears rolled down her cheeks as she stared at Tyler. "Can you forgive me?"

Tyler walked over to her. Looking down into her face, he saw simply his mother, nothing more, nothing less. Just the only mother he'd ever known. He put his arms around her and hugged her close, absorbing her cries with his body as he looked over her head and into the eyes of—his brother.

His brother...

"You say there's another one of us?" Tyler said softly.

John nodded. "And I think I know who and where he is. I need help, Tyler."

Julie got to her feet. She raised her champagne glass. "To new beginnings," she said, her gaze delving into Tyler's heart, "that tend to happen even when you're not looking for them."

Tyler picked up a glass and handed it to his mother, then took one for himself and clinked it against hers. "I'll drink to that," he said, and knew everything from this day on would be different and yet the same.

And that was okay.

* * * * *

Will they be able to find their brother?
Find out when THE LEGACY
comes to a heart-stopping conclusion next month!
Look for SOLDIER'S REDEMPTION
by Alice Sharpe wherever
Harlequin Intrigue books are sold!

COMING NEXT MONTH from Harlequin® Intrigue®
AVAILABLE JANUARY 2, 2013

#1395 STANDOFF AT MUSTANG RIDGE
Delores Fossen

After a one-night stand with bad boy Deputy Royce McCall, Texas heiress Sophie Conway might be pregnant with Royce's baby. And the possible pregnancy has unleashed a killer.

#1396 NATIVE COWBOY
Bucking Bronc Lodge
Rita Herron

When a selfless pregnant doctor becomes the target of a ruthless serial killer, she has no choice but to turn to the man who walked away from her months ago...the father of her child.

#1397 SOLDIER'S REDEMPTION
The Legacy
Alice Sharpe

Cole Bennett is at an impossible impasse: seek the truth of his past, though it threatens to destroy any chance of a future with the woman he loves, or turn away....

#1398 ALPHA ONE
Shadow Agents
Cynthia Eden

If Juliana James wants to stay alive, then she must trust navy SEAL Logan Quinn. But trusting Logan isn't easy...he's the man who broke her heart ten years before.

#1399 INTERNAL AFFAIRS
Alana Matthews

When Sheriff's Deputy Rafe Franco answers a callout on a domestic dispute, he has no idea that he's about to step into his past...and into the arms of the woman he had once loved.

#1400 BRIDAL FALLS RANCH RANSOM
Jan Hambright

Eve Brooks's beautiful face was erased by an explosion alongside a dark highway. But with former FBI agent J. P. Ryker's help, can she discover her inner beauty and strength before her tormenter strikes again?

You can find more information on upcoming Harlequin® titles, free excerpts and more at www.Harlequin.com.

HICNM1212

REQUEST YOUR FREE BOOKS!
2 FREE NOVELS PLUS 2 FREE GIFTS!

Harlequin

INTRIGUE

BREATHTAKING ROMANTIC SUSPENSE

YES! Please send me 2 FREE Harlequin Intrigue® novels and my 2 FREE gifts (gifts are worth about $10). After receiving them, if I don't wish to receive any more books, I can return the shipping statement marked "cancel." If I don't cancel, I will receive 6 brand-new novels every month and be billed just $4.49 per book in the U.S. or $5.24 per book in Canada. That's a saving of at least 14% off the cover price! It's quite a bargain! Shipping and handling is just 50¢ per book in the U.S. and 75¢ per book in Canada.* I understand that accepting the 2 free books and gifts places me under no obligation to buy anything. I can always return a shipment and cancel at any time. Even if I never buy another book, the two free books and gifts are mine to keep forever.

182/382 HDN FEQ2

Name _____ (PLEASE PRINT) _____

Address _____ Apt. # _____

City _____ State/Prov. _____ Zip/Postal Code _____

Signature (if under 18, a parent or guardian must sign) _____

Mail to the **Reader Service:**
IN U.S.A.: P.O. Box 1867, Buffalo, NY 14240-1867
IN CANADA: P.O. Box 609, Fort Erie, Ontario L2A 5X3

Not valid for current subscribers to Harlequin Intrigue books.

**Are you a subscriber to Harlequin Intrigue books
and want to receive the larger-print edition?
Call 1-800-873-8635 or visit www.ReaderService.com.**

* Terms and prices subject to change without notice. Prices do not include applicable taxes. Sales tax applicable in N.Y. Canadian residents will be charged applicable taxes. Offer not valid in Quebec. This offer is limited to one order per household. All orders subject to credit approval. Credit or debit balances in a customer's account(s) may be offset by any other outstanding balance owed by or to the customer. Please allow 4 to 6 weeks for delivery. Offer available while quantities last.

Your Privacy—The Reader Service is committed to protecting your privacy. Our Privacy Policy is available online at www.ReaderService.com or upon request from the Reader Service.

We make a portion of our mailing list available to reputable third parties that offer products we believe may interest you. If you prefer that we not exchange your name with third parties, or if you wish to clarify or modify your communication preferences, please visit us at www.ReaderService.com/consumerchoice or write to us at Reader Service Preference Service, P.O. Box 9062, Buffalo, NY 14269. Include your complete name and address.

HI11B

If thrilling romances and heart-racing action is what you're after, then check out Harlequin Romantic Suspense!

RS

NEW LOOK COMING DEC 18!

Featuring bold women, unforgettable men and the life-and-death situations that bring them together, these stories deliver!

HARLEQUIN®

ROMANTIC suspense

Four new stories available every month wherever books and ebooks are sold.

www.Harlequin.com

HRSPOST

COWBOY WITH A CAUSE
by Carla Cassidy

Turn the page for a sneak peek at the latest book
in the Cowboy Café miniseries

COMING JANUARY 2013!

HARLEQUIN®

ROMANTIC suspense

Heart-racing romance, high-stakes suspense.

HRSEXPINTRO1212